Vermeer's Lady in Waiting

Also by Lolly Anderson

How My Magic Refrigerator Sent Me to Paris Free

Aussie at the Skirvin Hilton

Vermeer's Lady in Waiting

Lolly Anderson

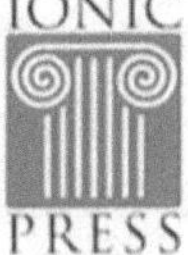

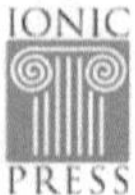

Vermeer's Lady in Waiting is a work of fiction.
The names, characters, places, and incidents are either
the product of the author's imagination
or are used fictitiously.
Any resemblance to actual persons, living or dead,
events, or locales is entirely coincidental.

Printed in the United States of America.

Cover design by Matt Goad.
Interior design by Margaret Gaeddert.

ISBN: 978-0-9819376-9-4 (Hardback)
ISBN: 978-0-9819376-8-7 (Paperback)

To Mike

the sine qua non of my everything

In memory of

Constance Fox Ingles

Prologue

Some places pull us into their orb with such beauty and power we cannot resist. Maybe a need deep within us is the magnetic force. Some people change our lives forever after one meeting. We may know them for years or only a short time. Art has that power I discovered.

A delicate painting I had known for years, or thought I knew, in my favorite place of beauty hid its dangerous secrets for fifty years. Then one day, one person, put me on a path that would change everything. I couldn't turn back. I couldn't run away. My only choice was to use all I had—body, mind, and spirit. Why didn't the psychic tell me I could lose my life?

There are many things I don't know. Except this: it is time for me to write the truth as I see it. It is time to quit worrying about who might sue me or not speak to me or not appreciate what I write. While we may debate the illusion of time and the mysterious transformative God-energy of love, we have only a finite number of days and moments to create, to tell our stories. It is time to tell mine regardless of the consequences.

Part One

"We live in a fantasy world, a world of illusion.
The great task in life is to find reality."
Iris Murdoch

1

National Gallery of Art
Washington, D.C.
2009

With the nation's Capitol in front of me, I walked down Constitution Avenue past the National Gallery of Art's palatial West Building, its white marble glowing in the morning light. The first cool breezes of fall had broken Washington's infamous sultry heat. Hope was in the air. A mere month ago I was hired at 'the Gallery' as I now called it, following my colleagues' lead. Would I be able to finesse my upbringing among the most sophisticated art professionals and collectors in the country? Would my ex-mother-in-law still say her precious son had 'married down' because my parents weren't the country club set? At least I had my luxury tags— my Tiffany watch and Christian Louboutin heels. My dear friend Luci once said of me, "Millicent has a magnetic personality, everything she has on is charged." And for now, that was still the case as far as my credit card use. Before I ruined my morning,

I ordered the negative out of my mind and focused on the iconic architecture around me.

Turning on Fourth Street, I entered the Gallery's East Building. The enormous Alexander Calder mobile moved gently overhead in the spacious atrium. I smiled as I showed my 'Millicent Clermont, Development' badge to the security officer.

"Good morning, Thomas. How is Shia?" I asked quietly.

"Doing much better, Miss Millicent. You didn't have to send that money, but we sure appreciate your kindness."

"It's the least I can do. Keep me posted." Thomas' three-year-old daughter faced several rounds of chemotherapy. Compared to that, my worries were nothing.

A special exhibition was being installed in the grand atrium. I gazed at the signature painting already in place, a seventeenth century work by Johannes Vermeer. The painting, *Mistress and Maid*, showed a woman wearing a fancy yellow jacket trimmed in white fur with small black markings. Her hair in a bun wrapped in tiny pearl strands complemented her pearl necklace and large pearl drop earrings. Her maid was handing her a letter, but the mistress did not seem eager to take it. Was it bad news? The painting's fine detail and delicate lighting made the world stand still as the mistress, interrupted from her writing, was caught in a moment of reflection.

Picturing the yellowed letters in my dresser at home,

I sighed and made myself move on to the day's work. I continued through the magnificent East Building, listening to how the grand space softened sounds, and entered the glass doors marked Administrative Offices. I flashed my ID and a smile to the seated guard and took the elevator to my office on the sixth floor.

Looking at today's date on my calendar, my heart tightened: October 2. The day Bill died. I had known him for only a year and yet his death still haunted me. Would I ever let him go?

Glancing back at my calendar, I was glad to see only one entry: 10:00 a.m. Member Lecture on Nazi Looted Art, East Auditorium.

Slipping into the ladies' room, I checked my round black glasses for smudges, fluffed my short hair, and reapplied my favorite coral lipstick, making sure my teeth weren't pink. By habit, I brushed off my black St. John suit, practically the Gallery uniform for development officers.

I made my way down the marble staircase and through the Modern and Contemporary Collections on my way to the lecture hall. So many artists, so many tortured lives. How many of them made a decent living? How many of them nearly starved to death? I hoped these artists could look down from heaven and see their paintings now hanging in one the most prestigious museums on earth. I passed Georgia O'Keeffe's *Shell* and then *Sea Battle* by Wassily Kandinsky, both heart and mind expanding. Monochromatic paintings, and the Gallery had quite a few, had yet to captivate me, an opinion I kept to myself. The Collections Committee, a donor group filled with collectors, gave thousands of dollars and then worked with Gallery curators to choose contemporary pieces to add to the museum's collection. As with all the art on permanent display at the Gallery, donors paid for its acquisition, not taxpayers. The annual federal government contribution kept the museum free to all visitors and open every day of the year except Christmas and New Year's. Close to five million people visited the National Gallery last year.

Glancing around the lecture hall to see if any of my donors were here—no—I sat down just in time. John Peale, the Gallery's director, approached the lectern. His silver hair and patrician look perfectly suited the man and the job. He might have come across as starched as his immaculate shirt with its gold collar pin, but after all he walked a tight wire under the scrutiny of unforgiving Washington politics. John Peale had to make sure there were no missteps that his many bosses—billionaire bosses called donors and high government officials called the Chief Justice of the United States Supreme Court and the Secretary of State, among others—could call him on. As uplifting to the mind and soul as the experience of art was, the business of art was a pressure cooker exacerbated in a federal government kitchen.

"Good morning and welcome to the National

Gallery," the director said as he adjusted the microphone. "We are fortunate to have with us Haywood Tabb of Tabb & Thomas. Mr. Tabb received his B.A. with honors in Art History from Princeton University and his J.D. from the University of Virginia. Mr. Tabb will discuss one of the thorniest issues facing museums today—Nazi looted art. Mr. Tabb."

Movie star handsome, Haywood Tabb flashed a bright smile that softened his serious white shirt and pinstriped suit. My obsessive love of movies took over to compare yet another person to a favorite actor. Denzel Washington or Will Smith? I eyed him closely as he waved to someone in the audience. Denzel. Yes, a young Denzel Washington.

"Thank you, John. It's a pleasure to be here," the lawyer said making eye contact across the room. "Everyone here has or had grandparents who worked hard and were good people. Perhaps your grandparents appreciated art and supported artists and museums because of their love of art.

"Now, imagine soldiers barging into their home and taking them away to the gas chambers. On top of that, these uniformed monsters stole every piece of art and valuable object in their home. You fortunately escaped the fate of your grandparents. But you inherited nothing except their love of art.

"Fast forward seventy years. You are visiting a museum. As you are touring the collection, you stop in your tracks. You are standing in front of a painting that hung in your grandparents' home. Now what do you do?

"This is when provenance research, or tracing the history of ownership of that painting begins. It is similar to a title search on a piece of land. What is different today is that research of a painting's chain of ownership—once done exclusively by museum curators—is now being done by individuals outside the museum world as well."

I double-checked my cell phone to make sure it was turned off and scanned the audience again. In front of me sat a couple who used to be all over me because they thought I could do something for them, in their case, host their company's Christmas party at the Gallery. After I told them the Gallery wasn't open to outside groups, I became invisible. Then I noticed across the room the woman of great wealth who treated me as her best friend until I declined her offer to run her foundation. At the last museum opening, she ignored me. How charming some people were when they thought you could help them with their agendas. Why did that disturb me so much? Because it reminded me of my ex-in-laws? My heavy sigh drew the attention of the person next to me. I put on my curious look and stared at the lecturer.

"After the fall of the Berlin wall in 1989 and the break up of the Soviet Union," Haywood Tabb continued, "hundreds of records and other documents became available for the first time. Several databases such as ArtLossRegister.com are now on the Internet to make provenance research faster and easier. Once you establish your right to possession, you present your claim. If the person or organization currently in possession does not surrender your grandparents' painting, you can file a lawsuit to recover it. That's where art restitution lawyers come in. Returning art to its rightful owners, or what we call art restitution, is my calling in life.

"Let me give you some background on Nazi looted art. Adolf Hitler considered himself a gifted artist and became enraged when the Vienna Academy of Arts rejected him. Once Hitler came into power, he and his henchmen stole thousands of works of art, mostly from Jewish families." Haywood's face darkened in anger. "Hitler's obsessive greed fed his plan to build a museum in his hometown of Linz, Austria. He felt entitled to rob private citizens of their artwork to fill his museum. His generals followed suit and were as greedy as Hitler. Fortunately for provenance researchers, the narcissistic Nazis kept copious records including photos and film, which help trace the journey a painting has taken.

"How Nazi Germany could value art—which lifts the human spirit to its highest expression—and yet devalue humankind to its lowest level is the paradox of the millennium."

Members of the audience nodded as Mr. Tabb's speech captured their attention. On the left aisle sat Richard Green, a Georgetown art dealer I had met years ago, wearing his signature green bow tie and handkerchief.

Art dealers, and he was no exception, were secretive, a different kind of 'Don't Ask Don't Tell' policy on what dealers would disclose about where their art inventory really came from. Some provenances were pure fiction.

"The millions of lives destroyed cannot be brought back," the lawyer said, took a sip of water, and resumed. "But at least, when a painting, sculpture, or other stolen art can be returned to its rightful owners, the past is redeemed in part. If any of you in the audience can identify and return one painting still missing from a family's estate, then you will know the satisfaction of participating in art restitution. Thank you."

The audience applauded and Haywood Tabb again flashed his luminous smile. Without knowing why, I walked up to introduce myself.

"Mr. Tabb, I'm Millicent Clermont with the Gallery. Interesting lecture." I shook his hand, cool and smooth. "I went to Virginia Law too. When were you there?"

"It's a pleasure to meet you, Millicent. I graduated in 2003. Great school. Great people. How did you choose Virginia?" he countered.

"Oh," I shrugged. "More to do with a person from Whittington than a studied career choice."

Haywood leaned in. "Did you say Whittington? Whittington Plantation?"

"Yes." My heart jumped at his words.

"My ancestors lived at Whittington," Haywood said looking directly at me.

"Gosh, what a coincidence." Goose bumps ran up my arms. "Would you like to go get a cup of coffee?"

"Absolutely," Haywood said, then glanced at the line that had formed behind me. "Give me about five minutes.

"I'll wait for you at the door." I nodded toward the lecture hall entrance.

Haywood turned to the next person in line, and I walked slowly up the steps amazed that this stranger had ties to my favorite place in the world. My whole being opened like a flower when I thought about Whittington.

Haywood finished chatting, picked up his briefcase, and met me.

"I can't believe you have a connection to Whittington," I pronounced as we strolled through the galleries and underground walkway.

"You must have a pretty strong connection yourself," Haywood said.

We picked up coffees at the Cascade Café and sat down across from I.M. Pei's glassed-in waterfall. The rush of water emitted a calming rhythm.

"I've been going to Whittington for over twenty years," I began, feeling my emotions expanding. "William and Lee Trevor bought the plantation in the sixties. I dated their oldest son. Bill was brilliant, musical, good-looking, so much like his mother. He was killed in a car accident his third year of law school at Virginia."

"I am so sorry." Haywood's voice was sincere.

"I was eighteen years old. It was the first time I was

in love. And my first experience of death."

"And you've never gotten over it," Haywood offered quietly.

Tears rimmed my eyes without my permission. "Bill's mother and I have stayed close all these years. In fact, Lee Trevor is the most important person in the world to me besides my parents. We don't agree on everything, but … Forgive me. I'm doing all the talking. Tell me about your ancestors."

"Nothing to apologize for. My great-grandparents six generations back lived at Whittington as slaves, of course, before the Civil War. My great-grandfather James worked in the fields. My great-grandmother Lela cleaned the house," Haywood said without embarrassment.

As he spoke I pictured James picking tobacco in one of the fields and Lela in the big white mansion cleaning the same dark hardwood floors I had walked many times. Haywood folded his napkin into a perfect square and positioned it under his coffee cup.

"I have wondered about Whittington," Haywood murmured gazing into the distance. "So it's still standing?"

"Absolutely. I would be happy to call Lee Trevor to arrange a visit. We could drive down together." The words popped out of my mouth before I had even thought about it.

"I would greatly appreciate it, Millicent, if it's not too much of an imposition. My sister lives in Norfolk and could come pick me up."

"Your sister would want to see Whittington too, wouldn't she?"

"Oh, no." Haywood shook his head. "My sister doesn't care to revisit the past. She thinks I'm crazy to want to trace our family's history. But it's who I am. 'The way to the future is through the past,' as Pierre de Chardin said."

"And I have found the way to the past is through the art." I handed him my card. "I'll call you as soon as I talk to Lee."

"Uh-oh, a fundraiser," Haywood said as he looked at my business card.

"It's a lot more fun than practicing law." And I meant it. There wasn't an adversarial bone in my body.

"For you maybe." Haywood rolled his eyes, lifted his briefcase with his initials embossed in gold, and turned toward the West Building.

Back in my office, I pulled my cell phone out to call Lee.

"Millie, darling. It is so good to hear your voice," Lee said, sounding like the *grande dame* she was.

"I met a lawyer who would like to see Whittington. Would you mind if we drove down next Saturday for a short visit?"

"I would love that. I do hope you can stay over. Is this a new beau I should know about?"

"No, no. Just another UVA lawyer. He wants to take

a quick look and then his sister is going to pick him up. Actually his ancestors…. Have I called at a bad time?"

"The Garden Club is here," Lee said over the noise of women's voices. "Fifty ladies for lunch. I'll have to call you later."

"Okay. Love you. Bye."

I gazed out my office window at the Capitol. The only African Americans I had ever seen at Whittington were the help. I should tell Lee that Haywood's ancestors lived as slaves at Whittington before I brought him to her front door.

2

Whittington Plantation
Gloucester County, Virginia

Haywood met me at my townhouse that next Saturday. He looked as crisp in his casual polo shirt and slacks as he did in his suit and tie. Lee and I had left each other phone messages but kept missing one other. I still hadn't told her why Haywood wanted to see Whittington.

"Great place," Haywood announced as he admired the front of my townhouse. "How long have you and your husband lived here?"

"Oh, no husband. So far death and divorce have kept me from living happily ever after," I shrugged lightly.

"How about you? Married with children?" I asked.

"Not yet. It's on the list. Afraid I've been married to my work."

We headed down I-95 South in my white Volvo. We would reach Whittington Plantation in three hours barring road construction. Whittington was as historic as it was remote. In 1676 after torching Jamestown,

Nathaniel Bacon set up headquarters at Whittington's closest neighbor, Warner Hall Plantation. A hundred years after that, troops on both sides of the Revolutionary War camped around both plantations before the decisive battle at Yorktown in 1781. During the Civil War General Robert E. Lee stayed at Whittington several times. In fact, Lee Trevor was a direct descendent of the General, hence her first name. I decided not to tell Haywood any of this.

"How did you get interested in art restitution?" I asked him.

"I've always loved art. I decided to go into art law after hearing the story of my roommate's great uncle who was an art dealer in Paris. After the Nazis stole his entire collection, he had no means of making a living. He was lucky to get out of Paris. After the war, he went back hoping he could recover his collection but he never did. What happened to him happened to countless European citizens. To this day, thousands of works of art stolen by the Nazis are still missing. Helping folks recover their cherished artwork is my small way of helping redeem the past." Haywood finished with fire in his eyes.

I turned onto 33 West toward Gloucester County happy we were that much closer to Whittington. "The only art restitution case I recall is when the National Gallery returned a Frans Snyders painting," I said. "I think it was in 2000."

"It was," Haywood said. "Snyders' *Still Life with Fruit*

and Game. An art dealer had given it to the museum in 1990. The National Gallery returned it to Madame Stern in Paris without a fight, which doesn't always happen. An Austrian woman by the name of Maria Altmann wasn't so lucky. She fought the Austrian National Gallery in court for years for her family's Gustav Klimt paintings the Nazis had confiscated. She was close to ninety years old when she finally won."

My naïve assumption that people would act enlightened around and about art was quickly disintegrating. Turning south on Route 17, my excitement ramped up since Whittington was only thirty minutes away.

"Millicent, when was the last time you visited Whittington?"

"Last spring." I took a deep breath. "It's a pilgrimage for me. A touchstone. Had I not met Bill, I would not have gone to Mary Baldwin College or to law school. I was headed to Oklahoma where my parents went to school. The Trevors have had a profound effect on my life. Lee Trevor is sophisticated, elegant, gracious …She's not perfect but I admire her tremendously."

"I'll try to be on my best behavior," Haywood said.

"Don't worry about that. I used to panic that Lee would never invite me back, that I had committed yet another *faux pas*. After twenty years I figured I could let go of my recurring fear."

I had released my deep-rooted fear but I was still

mortified about several things I did. Once I wore a large-brimmed purple hat through dinner at the long formal dining table. I hadn't washed my hair so the hat hid my unpresentable locks. Lee kept a perfectly straight face as we ate raw oysters she had served in silver cups on silver liners. My mother was horrified, absolutely horrified, when I told her. I was in college then, but still. A few years after that, I came barreling down the road, a real no-no because it created potholes, late for dinner, which made the food overcooked. And then afterwards, I rolled on the Persian rug in the front hall with Richmond ballet dancers there as guests. 'Interpretative dancing' the dancers and I had called it. That visit was filled with so many *faux pas*, I knew for certain *that was it, for sure* I would never be invited to Whittington again. But Lee always invited me back.

I realized I had been lost in my thoughts for several minutes.

"Tell me more about your family, Haywood."

"My great-grandmother Lela learned to read and write and taught her children, Midie and John, my great-grandfather five generations back. Midie and John were sold to another plantation. Unfortunately, Midie's beauty attracted the plantation owner. You can guess the rest. Part of our family is rather light-skinned, another Thomas Jefferson and Sally Hemmings scenario."

"Jumping forward, what led you to Princeton?" I asked.

"My family has always focused on education. My parents are lawyers. Their parents were teachers."

"In Virginia?"

"No, my grandparents taught at Fisk University in Tennessee. That's where my father grew up. Dad went to Columbia undergraduate and Columbia Law School where he met my mother. I was born in New York right after my parents got out of law school."

"Why didn't you stay up north?" I asked.

"Now you sound like a Southerner. Some of our family stayed in Virginia. I think it's the most beautiful state in the union."

"Spoken like the Yankee that you are." I grinned as I made the U-turn across Route 17 and turned right at the brick gate. "Haywood, we're here. This is Whittington," I said as I lowered my window. "And if you'll indulge me, let me describe our entrance. If I ever write a book, I will start with this phrase."

"Go for it," he said.

"It's a surprise—coming down the long lane through canopied trees and open fields, the house is—big, white, columned, nestled among old boxwood and ancient trees. The oldest tree of all, a golden gingko, sprinkles its fan-shaped leaves on the front porch hinting of the refinement within."

"Beautiful." Haywood said as he looked out both sides of the car.

We passed the small sign: "Slow Peacocks." The

afternoon sun illuminated the huge golden gingko and right on cue the house became visible all of a sudden.

"I can't believe I'm here," Haywood said under his breath.

I parked the car in the circular drive right behind Lee's old white Cadillac and we got out.

"Hi, George," I greeted the gardener nearby clipping shrubbery, his wrinkled black skin a stark contrast to his white hair.

"Fine, Miss Millie," he said, which wasn't the first time he had answered a question I hadn't asked. Haywood held up his hand acknowledging George with a faint smile.

We walked up the steps topped with pink geraniums in huge urns on either side. Never red flowers. Never yellow. I took a deep breath to smell the distinctive scent of the boxwood surrounding the porch. Traced to ancient Egypt, this delicate shrub was shipped from England to create formal gardens in the Colonies. While we waited for Lee to open the front door, I noticed paint peeling on the white columns and brick, worse than before. I pushed down my rising apprehension as to the wisdom of bringing Haywood here. I could hear Lee's footsteps inside and then she opened the door in a tailored blue sapphire dress setting off her slight frame. Her salt and pepper hair was thick as ever, her make-up minimalist, her eyes discerning. As obsessive as I was in comparing people to film actors, I had yet to find anyone I could compare to Lee.

"Millie, darling. I am so happy to see you." Lee hugged me.

"Lee, you look beautiful as always. This is Haywood Tabb." I held my breath looking for any sign of disapproval, but of course Lee had yet to learn that Haywood's ancestors had lived here. *Damn, I should have given Lee the full story before we showed up.*

"I am delighted to meet you," Lee said, smooth as honey. "Please come in and sit down. Would you care for a glass of wine?"

"Sounds wonderful." I answered for both of us.

"Great." Lee lightly clapped her hands together. "I'll be right back."

I exhaled as Haywood looked politely around the Williamsburg appointed room from circular staircase to the concert grand piano to the large framed paintings. I sat down in a wing chair and motioned for Haywood to sit on the camelback sofa.

"Lee has three house rules," I said, filling the time. "No drinks on the piano. And no one can remember the other two rules."

Lee reappeared with a silver tray carrying glasses of chilled wine. "Thank you," I said to Lee as I took a glass. *I had to tell her.* "Lee, Haywood's ancestors lived at Whittington in the late eighteenth century. That's why he wanted to see it." I searched Lee's face for her reaction. She either wasn't upset by the news or was hiding her feelings.

"How extraordinary, Haywood," Lee said, as she held the tray in front of him. "Do you know the dates?"

"Mrs. Trevor, first of all, thank you for allowing me to see Whittington." Haywood took a glass and held it on his knee.

"Please call me Lee." She sat in her Chippendale chair.

"Lee." He nodded. "My great-grandparents to the sixth degree, James and Lela, lived and worked on the plantation from 1790 until 1842. They were direct descendants of the first Africans brought to Hampton Roads, Virginia, in 1619 on the *San Juan Batista*. Our equivalent to the Mayflower Society."

I suppressed a laugh, because Haywood clearly meant it tongue-in-cheek. Lee didn't register a response.

"Then your ancestors were here when the house was expanded in 1790 by the Tabbs," Lee added and took a sip of wine.

"That's where my last name comes from, of course. The Tabbs were good to my family. Mrs. Tabb taught Lela to read and write."

"What a wonderful thing to learn about Whittington," Lee replied.

"When was the house built?" Haywood still held his glass on his knee.

"The main house was constructed in 1750," Lee answered. "The Tabbs doubled the number of bedrooms and built on the sun porch. Later my husband and I added the circular staircase and crown moldings."

"It's magnificent," Haywood said as he looked around the room. "Lela worked in the house. I guess she would have been in this room."

"This is so amazing." I took a sip of wine, relieved that the visit was going well.

"Let me show you the other rooms where Lela would have spent time." Lee rose from her chair.

We stood and followed her past the grand staircase and into the dining room. Flashes of my purple hat skipped through my mind. Lee led us into the living room. I could not look at this room without seeing Bill's purple draped casket that nailed our hearts to the floor twenty years ago.

"Do you play, Lee?" Haywood asked, gesturing at the gold harp in the corner of the dimly lit room.

"I used to," Lee said with a hint of resignation in her voice. "Many years ago. I only play the piano now."

After Bill died, Lee never played the harp nor wore jewelry except her rings.

"Lee could have been a concert pianist if she hadn't married," I said brightly. "And I've been awakened with a lively Chopin on more than one occasion after sleeping late." I looked affectionately at Lee. She had graduated from Bennington at the age of eighteen and then had earned a masters degree in music by age twenty. Small wonder Lee learned classical pieces with ease.

Haywood took in the high windows with damask

drapes now faded. Polished silver brightened the dark antique tables. We had entered the paneled library. The deep red leather wing chairs, the Williamsburg brass candlesticks, Lee's favorite Dutch painting over the fireplace. The library was a great place to spend an afternoon.

Haywood stepped over to the fireplace and looked immediately at the small painting over the mantle. It showed a woman in a pale blue jacket reading in front of a window, light streaming onto a black and white floor. Haywood searched it intently.

"Lee, this is a remarkable painting. If you don't mind my asking, was it purchased in Virginia?" Haywood had yet to take his eyes off the canvas.

"That is my favorite. I love the glow of the delicate light on the young woman as she intently reads the letter. You almost don't see it, but her face is reflected in the beveled glass. And look how the artist captured the sheen of her blue satin jacket." Lee sighed. "I adore it. My late husband gave it to me for my birthday. He bought it from a Washington art dealer. At a good price, knowing him. Millie, you remember meeting Richard Green at one of my parties, don't you?"

"How could I forget his green bow tie and matching handkerchief? In fact, I saw him last week. He attended the lecture Haywood gave at the Gallery."

"Oh, how interesting. I haven't seen Richard in years," Lee said.

"This looks so much like Vermeer's work," Haywood remarked, still peering at the woman in blue.

"I wish it were. There's no signature. Richard told us it was by a Dutch artist. That's all we've ever known."

"Vermeer did not sign all his paintings." Haywood continued examining every square inch of the diminutive work. And then with disquiet in his voice, "This looks exactly like a painting on the list of Nazi stolen art."

Lee looked as if Haywood had slapped her. I wanted to evaporate. I stopped breathing.

"I can assure you," Lee said sharply, "my husband would never have bought a stolen painting." Lee set her wine glass down and raised her head.

"Not knowingly, of course," Haywood quickly responded. "Few paintings or other works of art have a perfect provenance. I hate to be the one who tells you, but if your painting is the same Vermeer described in the Nazi looted art databases, it means a family in Europe is still searching for it."

"A painting by the famous Vermeer would not have been in our reach." Lee's voice was becoming colder with each word.

"Haywood, I'm sure you must be mistaken," I protested as I watched Lee stiffen. Her expression made it clear that this social call was over. My face turned oven hot. *Now I had committed the ultimate faux pas.*

Thankfully the sound of a car's engine and the crunch of tires on the gravel driveway shifted our attention. "That may be my sister," Haywood said, his tone of voice also flat.

"She's good at following directions," I blurted out in a false positive voice.

"Sarah's an engineer. She can find her way anywhere," he muttered as he turned away from the painting.

I walked toward the front door. An attractive woman was coming up the steps. Her beautiful skin and graceful walk made her a dead ringer for actress Halle Berry. Even in tense moments, my movie obsession worked overtime. I opened the door as Lee and Haywood came into the front hall. "You must be Sarah. I'm Millicent Clermont."

Haywood spoke next. "Mrs. Trevor, this is my little sister, Sarah Hunt."

"How do you do?" Lee said dully. No handshake. Nothing.

Sarah shot a knowing glance at Haywood. "We better go before the bridges become parking lots."

"Mrs. Trevor, thank you." Haywood did not try to take Lee's hand.

I bit my lip as I followed Haywood down the steps and out to his sister's car. After Lee closed the front door, I exploded. "Haywood, I can't believe you, you..." I couldn't find the words I was so mad. "This is mortifying!"

"I'm sorry. But I couldn't remain silent."

"The Trevors never had that kind of money. Not the kind to buy a Vermeer," I said angrily then realized that Lee might hear our conversation.

"Check out ERRproject.org. You'll find a listing of a Vermeer painting. See if you don't think it's the same painting."

"What is the ERR?" I asked still angry but not as loud.

"The ERR was the notorious Nazi agency that plundered art in Nazi-occupied countries."

"And you saw Lee's painting on this site?"

"Yes."

"So Lee is just supposed to give away her favorite possession?"

"First, the painting has to be examined to verify its provenance. But, Millicent, you may have a hand in returning it to a grateful family. Sooner or later they are apt to file a lawsuit. I don't think Mrs. Trevor wants to wait until it gets to that point."

"Haywood, can you discuss this later?" Sarah raised her beautiful eyebrows. "I really want to get out of this place."

Haywood looked at his sister and then back at me. "I've got a big case this week. I'll call you as soon as I can."

I solemnly waved goodbye, wishing I had never laid eyes on the man. My footsteps were heavy as I went back inside, dreading the rest of the weekend.

3

Whittington Plantation
Georgetown

After my apology for Haywood's bombshell, Lee changed the subject immediately. That was the end of that. There were certain topics never discussed and Lee had added this to her list. We had a pleasant enough dinner but there was an unspoken tenseness. I hated being in this situation. How could a simple gesture to show someone where his ancestors had lived turn into this horrible situation? I went to bed early, not my usual custom at Whittington, telling Lee I had to leave in the morning.

In the middle of the night I woke up, wide awake. I turned on the small lamp next to the bed. The yellow glow brought the elegant room into faint focus. The antique high chest with its brass pulls stood against the wall as if things were the same as before. But nothing was the same. Sliding out of the four-poster bed, I put on my glasses, carefully opened the bedroom door and tiptoed down the circular staircase. The house was quiet, soundless except for the soft chiming of the grandfather clock. A circle of light from the side table in the front hall made it easy to slip into the library.

I switched on the chandelier, slowly closed the door, and dropped into the dark red leather chair. I stared at the Dutch painting. I wondered about the woman in her blue satin jacket reading her letter. Where did she come from? Where had she been? I took off my glasses, now becoming sleepy, and dozed off.

How long I was asleep I do not know. But the dream I had burned into my brain. A Nazi general was slapping his gloves against his hand, strutting through a beautiful apartment filled with art. "The Fuehrer will be pleased," he said. Then a young blond officer appeared in the elegant living room and pointed to a painting on the wall. Lee's painting. "This is the best one of all!" The general ordered his aide to take the painting down and deliver it to the Jeu de Paume. The aide's arm became a flying oar as he saluted, "Heil, Hitler!" As the aide turned to go, the general shot him. His blond hair fell into his eyes as he tumbled to the floor. The general grabbed the painting, Lee's painting, and cut the canvas out of its frame. He rolled it up and jammed it in to his jacket. With his black shiny boots clicking, he strolled out of the grand home.

I woke up in a sweat. What a strange dream. What a vivid dream. I looked up at the Dutch painting and rushed out of the library.

The next morning Lee and I hardly spoke as I left Whittington, digging a huge hole in my heart. I turned north onto Route 17 with a dozen questions, steps in quicksand, pulling me into a mire. Had the Trevors known that Nazis had stolen the painting? Not Lee. What if Lee had to give up her favorite painting? If she did give it up, how would she be compensated? Good deeds all of a sudden became completely theoretical. Did Richard Green, the art dealer and supposed friend of the Trevors, know it was stolen art? And a lawsuit? That would cost Lee thousands of dollars.

This woman's approval was oxygen to me. Losing her love would be the worst thing that could ever happen. As long as I felt accepted by Lee, I could handle any rejection, any disappointment in life. Was it because she and her son had invited me into their world when I was only seventeen years old, before I became a lawyer? If Bill had lived, would we have married? I didn't know. But with his death, Bill gave me his mother. Our relationship kept Bill alive. It was something we both needed.

I reached Georgetown, found a parking place close to my townhouse on N Street— a miracle—and immediately called my next-door neighbor. I needed to vent.

"Andrew, it's Millicent. Are you going to be home for a few minutes?"

"Millicent, dah-ling, what a nice surprise. Yes, I shall be here."

Pulling myself up the steps to Andrew's townhouse, I tapped the brass doorknocker. The heavy black door swung open.

"Come in, Millicent. Lovely day," Andrew greeted me, dressed immaculately as usual, in starched shirt and pants. He kissed me on the cheek and waved me in. An older version of Jude Law with a Southern accent, Andrew Barlowe's reputation as the finest writer for *The Washington Post* was matched only by his eccentricity. His home looked as if he had taken a large antique shop and fit it all into his much smaller townhouse. "Faded Anglo-Saxon gentility at its zenith," was the way Andrew described it. Numerous crystal chandeliers, silver on every surface including the kitchen counters, oil paintings hung floor to ceiling even in the bathrooms: it was an unforgettable *pied-a-terre.*

His bedroom, which he had made into a large walk-in-closet with a daybed, included the correct outfit for every social occasion imaginable all neatly arranged wall-to-wall according to type and color. The expression 'close to the vest' was literally true, at least as far as his sleeping arrangement. Andrew's style of dress was the look that Ralph Lauren's billion-dollar business was built on. His calendar overflowed with invitations to formal parties and dances. Andrew was often the most attractive person man or woman at any soiree. He was a writer at heart, a

Southern society gentleman by birth.

"Hold on, doll, let me get a cigarette. Would you care for a cummerbund?"

Andrew's 'cummerbund' was his invention of vodka and soda with a slice of cucumber.

"Yes, thank you," I said as I gingerly tiptoed around the tables artfully covered with priceless antiques. Passing my favorite rose damask chair, I sat in my designated seat, the leather wing chair facing a seventeenth century game table covered in a sea of silver. Andrew handed me my drink and sat where he always did, in the cracked brown leather wing chair on the other side of the table. His signature black Bic lighter ignited the tip of a Marlboro.

"Andrew, something terrible has happened."

"What on earth, Millicent?" Smoke twirled in the air around his head.

"An art restitution lawyer is convinced that a Dutch painting at Whittington is a stolen Vermeer. Lee's favorite painting!"

"Oh, my," Andrew tapped his cigarette on his vintage beanbag ashtray. "Why does he think so?"

"He said it's on the list of Nazi looted art. Reading about other cases of stolen art returned to the original owners always hit me as wonderful stories. Now that it's close to home, I see it so differently. Lee might lose something she has cherished for years. And if she doesn't do something soon, she might get sued."

"But you don't know for sure it was stolen."

"No, we won't know until it's examined. And of course I don't want Lee to keep anything that belongs to someone else. But how is she going to be compensated?" I took a gulp of the vodka drink.

"Now calm down, dah-ling. Don't you remember the story in 2000 about the Rubens painting that had been traded by Hitler's art dealer, Karl Haberstock, and was assumed to have been stolen? It was all over the papers and they were wrong."

"No, I don't remember." I missed many things because of my divorce.

"It was true that the Rubens portrait passed through the hands of Haberstock," Andrew continued, "but it was eight years before the Nazis came to power."

"I don't want to deal with this." I took another swallow of my drink.

"Yes… life…" Andrew put out his half finished cigarette and moved the ashtray to the floor beside his chair. "Glorious life. Happy. Sad. One challenge after another. I've a challenge of my own. With the way newspapers are going, I will be out of a job in the not too distant future."

"Andrew, that can't happen. You are one of the top writers at *The Post*."

"But it can. Look what happened at *The Chicago Tribune*. Even Sam Zell couldn't save it." Andrew took out another cigarette, looked at it, and put it back in the pack. And then sipped his cummerbund.

"It would be tragic if newspapers went out of business," I exclaimed, speaking from my heart as much as from the vodka. "Terrible if we lose the ritual of reading the paper with a cup of coffee. I love to roll my eyes over words on paper. Words are the jewels of our existence. Words lure us into new worlds, their juxtaposition the treasure of our lives." The actress in me leaned back in my chair, performance over.

"What is a ritual for you, Millicent, is my life line. But we are witnessing the end of an era. The end of civilization as we have known it." Andrew shook his head with a resigned look and took out the same cigarette he had replaced a moment ago.

"Want to go to Bistro Lepic tonight?" I proposed, hoping to perk us up. Bistro Lepic was my favorite French restaurant not far on Wisconsin Avenue.

"I would love to but my friend from Palm Beach shall be arriving tonight and has invited me to the Sulgrave Club. Let's lunch next week at Cosmos."

"Yes, let's do." I rose feeling every ounce of the cummerbund drink and gazed at the full-length portrait of his mother à la John Singer Sargent's *Madame X*. "Don't get up. And thanks for listening to my tirade, Andrew. See you later." I blew him a kiss and slipped out.

"Take care now, dah-ling."

I stepped onto the cobblestone sidewalk, took the dozen steps to my townhouse, and let myself in. Before the darkness ate up the minimal light coming from the chandelier in the foyer, I flipped on another light switch. I filled a glass with ice then water, put some leftover pasta in the microwave, and looked through my DVDs. I needed something light and funny. I popped *French Kiss* with Kevin Kline and Meg Ryan into my living room DVD player. Let the therapy begin. I always cried hearing its sound track, especially "Someone Like You" by Van Morrison, but a good cry would do me good. Thank heavens I had a busy week coming up, a trip to Boston, and a visit to a psychic.

4

Boston

As the plane came in for landing at Logan Airport, I looked out the window at the quilted mounds of tiny buildings. As the sun hit the rooftops of the miniature structures, they looked like dozens of pieces of white Chiclets gum. I dreaded the ride from the airport through the infamous tunnel, but meeting a potential donor who wanted to give the National Gallery a painting made it worth it. First on the agenda was a visit to the Isabella Stewart Gardner Museum. Part of being a good development officer was educating oneself about art and museums.

Entering the Gardner Museum, I viewed the John Singer Sargent full-length portrait of Mrs. Gardner in the foyer and thought of Andrew's mother.

"Isabella Stewart Gardner fashioned her museum after a fifteenth century Venetian villa," the director, a smartly dressed woman with a slight Boston accent, pointed out as she led me through the interior courtyard filled with flowers and greenery. "The second century mosaic floor in the middle of the courtyard was shipped from Rome in pieces and reconstructed." The director gestured up. "Mrs. Gardner lived on the fourth floor. She made her museum into a cultural jewel, filling it with great art and entertaining famous artists and musicians."

I imagined Isabella in her Victorian clothing and then in the latest Parisian fashions, as she was schooled in Paris, when she opened her museum to the public in 1903.

"In 1990," the director said with a frown, "thieves posing as policemen talked their way into the museum, tied up the security guards, and stole millions of dollars worth of art: three Rembrandts, five Degas, a Manet, and a Vermeer, among other priceless works."

I shook my head in disbelief. Theft was rampant in the art world, but this heist was particularly offensive. Although Mrs. Gardner had died in 1924, this break-in was a personal violation of a generous woman. It depressed me that Johannes Vermeer's *The Concert,* one of only thirty-five known paintings by the artist, was still lost. It was mind boggling that my mentor Lee Trevor might have a Vermeer, and on top of that, a Vermeer that had been stolen by the Nazis. I spent a few more minutes exploring this gem of a museum by myself and left, as I always did from a museum, in a more relaxed state.

Next on my agenda was the appointment with Theodore Pennington who wanted to give a painting to the Gallery. He lived in the Back Bay on the corner of

Beacon Street and Gloucester. In 1850, the Back Bay was a swamp along the Charles River before becoming the largest landfill in Boston. Now it was of one of the most fashionable neighborhoods in America. Mr. Pennington arrived at the same time I did so we greeted each other at the front door of his handsome 1925 building, considered new among its nineteenth century neighbors.

"Miss Clermont, so nice to meet you." His round wire glasses fogged up a bit. "Let's go up and have a glass of sherry."

He led me through the lobby with its beautiful coffered ceiling and into the paneled elevator. Stepping out on the third floor into his apartment, Mr. Pennington opened his closet door, wadded his coat into a ball, and threw it onto the top shelf. His spacious flat, although appointed with English antiques and a nice art collection, bore the mark of a mad professor who cared little about appearances.

"Mr. Pennington, you are so generous to want to give a painting to the Gallery. Much less a painting by Matisse."

"Well, if they want it." He poured two small glasses of sherry. "You see, my mother left it to me. As you can tell, I don't have a place to properly honor it." He went into another part of his apartment and brought back a colorful, whimsical canvas showing a woman sleeping, her head resting on a table, typical of Henri Matisse's child-like compositions.

"What a great piece and a great addition this will be

to the Gallery's collection. Of course, the curatorial staff at the Gallery will have to approve its acceptance. But once that happens, you will receive a letter that will result in a handsome tax deduction," I said.

"Yes, yes. I understand. I'm going to have the painting appraised, you see, and then bring it to Washington myself. It has an exciting history. The German army plucked it during the war and took it to the Jeu de Paume museum. Then Hermann Goering, Hitler's right hand man, took it from the Jeu de Paume on one of his many shopping sprees. Goering didn't want it. He hated this sort of art. He took it to trade for something else. The painting eventually was returned to the original art dealer the Germans stole it from and then changed hands many times before my mum bought it."

I thanked Theo, as we were now on a first name basis, and told him I looked forward to his visit. True, I was new at the Gallery, but I had visited countless museums in my life. I had never been aware of Nazi stolen art and now the subject had come up twice in one week.

My last appointment was my visit to a psychic. As I strolled down Beacon Street, sunlight dappled the leaves as if I had stepped into a Renoir painting. My Donald Pliners shoes softened the cobblestone pavers. I moved freely in my knit suit. Then a clear image came to me. I was on these same cobblestones in a heavy dress with bustle and thin leather shoes. It was an image and a feeling, a feeling of *déjà vu*. But more. The dainty pumps and whalebones under linen camisole and petticoats seemed more real than the stretchy skirt and cushy shoes I was wearing. I stopped and shook my head to regain my composure. I must start eating more protein.

I continued toward the big "T" sign and rode the subway to Harvard Square. The psychic's office was located right off the square at 10 Charles Street. My best friend Gabby had recommended Diane Miles because Diane used astrology along with her psychic abilities, and Gabby had been astonished at what Diane had told her. Nancy Reagan and Princess Di had consulted psychics. And Carl Jung was a proponent of astrology. So I was in good company. The only information I had provided to Diane beforehand was the place and exact time of my birth.

I knocked on the door wondering what this adventure was going to produce.

An attractive blond opened the door. "Millicent? Hi, I'm Diane." She ushered me in into her well-appointed office. Not the typical fuzzy brown psychologist cave. With her tailored suit and professional demeanor, she could easily have passed for a lawyer. So much for stereotypes. I sat on the couch where she indicated.

"First I'm going to give you your birth chart," Diane said as she handed me a document with a circle divided into twelve equal parts. Symbols and lines filled the spaces. "This is a picture of the sky the moment you were born. Your sun sign is Aquarius, your rising sign is Sagittarius, and your moon is Cancer. You have to know all three signs to get an accurate reading, like the three points of a triangle. Horoscopes in the newspaper are pretty meaningless because only the sun aspect is given."

"What does the rising sign mean?"

"That is your persona, your face to the world. It's not what really makes you tick, that's your sun sign."

"And the moon? What does that refer to?"

"That is a person's emotional base. With yours in Cancer, sometimes your emotions take over your core energy of Aquarius, which is analytical. We'll talk about this later after we go through a regression. Have you done a regression before?"

"No, I haven't."

"Let me explain how it works. First, I lead you into a meditative state. Then we will explore the different phases in your soul path. It is important to be still so the messages you receive will be clear."

I lay back on the couch thinking of *New Yorker* cartoons and took three deep breaths as instructed.

"As you exhale, let go of all tensions and thoughts. Completely relax," Diane said.

I felt a bit apprehensive but followed her instructions. After all, I was spending two hundred and fifty dollars an hour.

After a minute or so she began. "Now I want you to describe your birth."

How could I describe my birth? Okay, I decided to play along. "I was born at a military hospital in San Antonio. My father was a pilot in the Air Force. My grandparents were there; my whole family was there." Actually in the back of my mind, I had a feeling no one was there except my mother and me.

"How long did you stay in the hospital?"

"I don't think we were there that long. A couple of days," I guessed.

"Now it is the year 1900. Tell me where you are."

Oh, boy. This was going to be good. If I was born in San Antonio, then I figured I would have been somewhere near Texas.

"I am hovering over Texas, waiting to be born," I continued my charade.

"Good. Now it is the year 1885. Where are you now?"

I mean, really. I was making this up. But, if I ever did live another life, I would have lived in a townhouse on a cobblestone street in a place like Boston or Georgetown; it's where I feel most at home. I told her that.

"Yes," Diane nodded. "But not Boston or Georgetown. You lived in England in the nineteenth century."

A strange calm came over me. Maybe I did live in England. It rang so true. I thought of my love of antique silver and late Victorian clothing, my strong desire to buy a vintage dress, one with a bustle and high neck. What about the *déjà vu* experience I had had thirty minutes ago?

"Were you married in England?" Diane inquired.

"Yes," I said hesitantly. More make-believe here. Then a man's face, a man I had dated, flashed in my head. He was a lawyer who bought his suits in London and took me to dinner in Georgetown at a private club founded in 1842. If he was from my past life, who else was? When we had an immediate attraction to people, was it because we had known them in a past life? This was totally bizarre.

"Now it is the year 1790, where are you?" The psychic's voice was quiet but strong. I felt an agitation in my chest and I saw the color red as if my chest was covered in red. Red blood. *My* red blood. But I wasn't a woman. I was a man. A soldier in a red and blue uniform with gold braid. A French soldier.

"You were the son of a prominent businessman who fought on the French-German border."

All kinds of thoughts raced through my head. My love of all things French. My many Francophile friends. My negative reaction to things German, except for cars and coffee makers.

"You were rich and arrogant like someone in your past. Someone you pulled in to work out your issues of money."

"That would be my ex-husband," I muttered.

"That marriage helped you form a healthy ego," Diane explained. "And you will use that anger toward your ex-husband and his parents in a positive way someday. It was also your money lesson. You see how money and materialism lead people astray, away from their true nature and make them selfish and unfeeling toward others."

Her words had the force of truth.

"You will marry again. A man who is already at the top of his field. A man who gives you the security you have always searched for. That is why that plantation means so much to you. It represents the stability you thought you never had. That's why you went to a historic college. You desperately needed roots. Someday you will settle down and fulfill the purpose God put you on earth to accomplish."

How could she know about Whittington unless she truly was psychic? I had never mentioned Whittington Plantation or Lee Trevor to her. I hadn't mentioned my terrible marriage and divorce. "I am dating a writer now. He's very successful. Is he the one?"

"Before your love life comes together, Saturn, the planet of hard lessons, will square Uranus, the planet of change, in your birth chart and present you with the challenge of your life," she said.

"What kind of challenge?" I asked.

"I don't know exactly. It has to do with art. What do you do? Are you an artist?"

"No. I raise money for the National Gallery of Art."

"Well, it will involve," Diane tapped her pen on the desk, "people at the highest levels of government in the United States and Europe. I don't know what that would be."

"Oh, great. Good news, bad news." I sighed.

I wrote out a check for Diane's fee and walked out into the bright sunlight deep in my revelations.

When I returned to my hotel I called my mother and asked her about my birth.

"We were stationed in Austin, but the base there didn't have a hospital," she told me. "So your father drove me to the army hospital in San Antonio. And um, we stayed only a couple of days after you were born." My mother had taken to adding 'and um' to practically every sentence.

"My grandparents didn't come to the hospital?" I asked surprised.

"No, Millie. It would have taken them an entire day to get there. It was only the two of us. Then your father came and picked us up. When we got home, he told me he had orders and we would be leaving in six weeks for Alaska." That my grandparents weren't at the hospital didn't bother me. I knew they loved me. I was taken aback that my feelings during the psychic session were true to the actual events.

After I hung up, I went to the Boston Public Library in Copley Square not far from my hotel. I looked in a book on 'Military Uniforms' and then looked under 'French Soldiers.' I expected to confirm my impression they wore only blue and white uniforms. I did find pictures of soldiers in blue and white military garb, but to my surprise, also red and white, and red and blue. It depended on their regiment. The French regiments fighting the Germans wore red and blue uniforms. Maybe there was something to this psychic business.

5

National Gallery of Art
Washington, D.C.

The psychic's predictions about my pending challenges were on my mind, like a bird perched on my head, as I made the power walk down Constitution Avenue to the Gallery. I passed the West Building and marveled at John Russell Pope's creation, the largest marble building in the world when it opened in 1941. Six-thousand guests were invited; eight-thousand people showed up to hear President Roosevelt accept the late Andrew Mellon's gift to the nation. What a shame Mr. Pope had died too, before the dedication.

Once on Fourth Street, I entered the white angular East Building, which was designed by I.M. Pei and opened in 1978. Leaving the morning's gasoline fumes and impatient honks behind me, the muted hushed sounds in the grand atrium calmed me.

I closed my office door and changed from my walking

shoes into heels. After a frustrating hour calling prospects to set up one-on-one meetings to no avail, I decided to take a break and Google 'provenance research.' Two hours glued to my computer screen flew by. I glanced at my watch, glad it was time for lunch with Andrew Barlow.

The Cosmos Club on Massachusetts Avenue was a cab ride away. Its members were serious authors, high government officials, and other powerful elite. Andrew wore his signature oxfords, pink shirt, and on his suit lapel, his Society of the Cincinnati rosette signifying he was a direct descendent of an officer in George Washington's army. He kissed me on the check and guided me to the buffet. We sat down at a table near the window with our plates.

"I've been reading about provenance research," I announced.

"Fascinating, Millicent, absolutely fascinating," Andrew deadpanned as he repositioned his flatware before starting to eat.

"Well, really it is. I read more about what you had mentioned, that an art piece might appear to have been looted when in fact there was a legitimate sale. Apparently there are three initial tests provenance researchers look for. First, was there a gap in ownership of Lee's painting from 1933, when Hitler came to power, until the end of the war in 1945? Two, was Lee's painting in Europe during this time? Finally, was the painting sold or traded by any art dealer on the 'red flag" list who handled looted art?"

"Seems you're on the right track."

"I hope so, Andrew. I hope so."

The rest of the meal we chatted about Andrew's next party and who was going to be there. Andrew was one degree of separation from people who vacationed with British royalty.

Former SEC Commissioner Isaac Hunt came up to the table to say hello. I became acquainted with Commissioner Hunt after he gave a series of lectures at UVA law school. He was the second African American to graduate from the law school in 1959. Andrew knew him from a piece he did on the Securities and Exchange Commission. Ike always looked as if he had stepped out of GQ magazine, as he should, since he had his suits custom made on Wisconsin Avenue next to Bistro Lepic. He was handsome but sad; the same week he was confirmed by the U.S. Senate, his wife died of a heart attack.

Andrew signed his ticket and we parted at the door.

I sat down in my office chair when the phone rang.

"Millicent, can you come up? I need to see you. Now." The Gallery director's voice was firm.

"Sure, John. I'll be right there." The director had never called me to his office in this way. My face flushed as I walked up the white-carpeted stairs to the seventh floor, bright light pouring into the stairwell from the I.M. Pei skylight. The executive suite of one of the most prestigious museums in the world emanated power and authority.

"Go right in, Millicent," Amy, the director's assistant said, her eyes on high alert.

I approached the threshold, my heart pounding.

"Come in, Millicent. Please close the door and have a seat."

Should I sit in the sofa or in one of the club chairs? I took the sofa and tried to calm my thumping heart.

John Peale rose from his desk chair, buttoned his suit jacket, and curtly handed me some papers before sitting in one of the club chairs.

"What's this about? It's all over the Internet." The director's voice was gruff.

My face burned as I read the headlines in the online magazine article:

NATIONAL GALLERY STAFF HIDES NAZI LOOTED ART, OWNERS SUE FOR RETURN

I looked up at John in a panic. Rupert Murdoch's *News of the World* hacking scandal shot into my thoughts. Had someone hacked into my phone or had Haywood betrayed me?

"I can't believe this. This is outrageous. I took Haywood Tabb to Whittington Plantation, the home of my mentor, Lee Trevor. Haywood saw Mrs. Trevor's Dutch painting and said it looked like a Vermeer listed in a Nazi looted art database. I'm in complete shock. I can't believe Haywood did this to me." I looked down at the article again but the lines became blurry I was so mad. How could Haywood have done this?

"The art world is a small universe. When valuable works of art are on the move, people talk," John Peale said, his face rigid. "Have you been served with a petition?"

"No. John. I'm completely blindsided."

"Well, so am I." His face was turning a mad red. "You need to go see Legal. And you'd be smart to hire your own lawyer."

I realized I had stopped breathing. I took a breath and sat back. How could things go wrong so fast? "How would this online magazine know any of this when we haven't even been notified?"

"An aggressive reporter poking around the courthouse desperate for a story, or the strategy of the plaintiff's lawyer positioning for a larger fee. Not that that matters now." The director stood. Meeting over. "See if Mrs. Trevor will let us examine the painting."

I stood. "You mean take it from Lee?" I muttered, breathless.

"If the painting is here at the Gallery, we can determine if it is a real Vermeer and the same painting that's missing. Congress is going to go nuts over this. It could jeopardize our funding, Millicent. And cost you your job."

Tears welled up in my eyes as I stumbled out of the

director's office. I ran down the white stairs and quickly closed my office door. My emotions overtook me. I had been thrilled to get this job, thankful to be getting my equilibrium back after the divorce. Now *this*. Was Haywood taking out some sick revenge on Whittington? What should I do first? Hire a lawyer? Call Lee?

6

Whittington Plantation
Georgetown

Gloomy skies matched my mood as I drove to Gloucester County to ask my revered mentor to give me her painting. My experiences of Whittington flashed before me. The first time Bill brought me to Whittington, I felt like Cinderella: his parents' formal dinner party, a black waiter in starched coat that could stand on its own serving me wine, our early morning intimacies in the guest bedroom, chaste by today's standards. My second visit: seeing his casket draped in purple velvet that cut my life into *before* and *after.*

Months after Bill's death, Lee had called to invite me to Whittington for Easter. I had been surprised by her invitation. At Bill's funeral another female, obviously a girlfriend, was so visibly upset that the family had to tend to her during the service. Nothing, with the exception of losing Bill, could have devastated me more. I had seen Bill a mere week before he died. We had made plans to get together in Charlottesville. What about all those letters he had written me? Years later Bill's sister told me the family had been furious at this other girlfriend for making such a fuss.

Other trips to Whittington came to mind. The blissful spring weekend when I took the first swim of the season in the icy cold swimming pool as cows out of their fence mooed nearby. The Christmas right after my divorce when I was so sad and so thin. The thin part I loved. The elegant parties at neighboring plantations. Being awakened in the morning by Lee playing Chopin. Dancing around the front hall with ballerinas from the Richmond Ballet after dinner. And of course the purple hat.

Now I had to tell the person I put on a pedestal that she must give up her favorite painting and was in the middle of a costly lawsuit. All because of me, because I had brought a stranger to Whittington who turned on us for his own personal gain.

All my reminiscing made the miles roll by. I had reached Whittington.

Turning into the lane, I lowered my windows despite the light rain and turned off the radio. The canopied trees sheltered most of the rain and gave off a clean green fragrance. In the open fields, the sun sent a shaft of light through the raindrops giving the appearance of glass beads hanging in a giant doorway. The wet magnolias glistened dark green. The house peeked behind the voluminous foliage then dropped its cover in an instant. How could it look so peaceful?

I opened my Monet umbrella and quickly ran up the stone steps. The boxwood emitted its romantic fragrance. I knocked on the door and tried to open it. Locked. The rain had stopped. I felt around the side of the house to get the heavy brass key Lee hid for expected guests.

As I turned the key, a beautiful antique weighing several ounces, I saw myself in Victorian clothing again.

I had managed to open the door when I heard the crunch of gravel and turned around to see Lee driving up.

Lee parked her car and lowered her window. "Sorry I'm late. The rain was dreadful."

She looked as if she had aged ten years since I last saw her. I went down the steps to help her out of the car. "Are you all right, Lee?"

"No, Millie, I'm not."

"What's the matter?" I asked cautiously as we slowly managed the steps.

Lee didn't answer me until we were inside. "I've been in Richmond meeting with tax lawyers. I had received a letter from the I.R.S. I'm afraid I'm … well, no one's going to die, but I …" Lee's voice trailed off as she sat down in the Chippendale chair by the piano.

I was stunned to hear Lee talk this way. Physical maladies were rarely discussed. Money never.

"May I get you something to drink?" I asked her.

"No, no. I'll be fine. Let me rest for a minute."

"I'll get you a glass of water." I returned to the front hall to find Lee exactly in the same position. "So you have a big tax bill?" I was mortified to ask about anything financial. How was I going to tell her about the lawsuit?

"For fifteen million dollars," Lee said distantly looking straight ahead.

"Fifteen million dollars? You're kidding." I sank into the sofa.

"You know, I never delved into my husband's business affairs," Lee said. "He left for Washington for the week and came home on the weekends. I knew he had many business interests, but he never talked about them. When he died, I had to sell some of the land to pay estate taxes. But I owe more. A lot more. Something about limited partnerships that were sold. I have no way of ever paying this kind of money."

"Maybe it's a mistake, Lee. The I.R.S does make mistakes."

"I'm afraid not. My lawyers looked over the audit. Since the taxes weren't paid, the penalties are enormous. I have no idea what will happen to Whittington."

"Lee, I am so sorry." What was I going to do? How could I give her more bad news?

"Shall I fix us some roast beef sandwiches and maybe a Bloody Mary?" Lee offered, being the consummate hostess.

"Yes, some protein will do us some good." I needed more time to figure out my approach. Thank heavens for social graces that took over in the midst of crisis.

I followed Lee to the kitchen. The peacocks picked around outside the window among the boxwood, their colorful tails trailing behind them, oblivious to our stunned state of mind. I nervously paced the kitchen as Lee fixed a beautiful tray with our lunch. She carried it to the library, the room chosen when weather was inclement, my eyes on her delicate back.

"Oh, we won't want to eat in here," she remembered.

I looked at the blank wall, the sooty outline where the painting had hung over the mantel. "Lee! Where's the painting?" I blurted. "Oh, no!" I fell into the red wing chair. "That's why I came."

"I don't understand," Lee looked at me completely puzzled.

"Apparently Haywood was right. Your painting does look similar to the one on the list of stolen art. But I'm afraid there's something else. We've both been sued over it."

Lee plunked the tray on the green felt tablecloth. I thought she was going to faint. She plopped into the nearest chair. "The tax bill. Now this. My world is falling apart."

"Lee, I don't know what to say. I feel terrible. It's all my fault." My hands were on my face.

"It's not your fault, Millie. But I don't know what is to be done."

"Where is the painting?" I asked, my voice cracking. "The director of the National Gallery told me to ask you if the Gallery could examine it."

"It's gone. I gave it to the art dealer, Richard Green. That painting and a few others." Lee stared at the rug. "He told me he could help me out. I was… I am desperate. If I don't come up with some funds for the I.R.S., I could lose Whittington."

My mind felt dead as I drove back to D.C. I wanted to go home and hide. I would have given anything to turn back the clock. What was I going to tell the director? Was Lee going to lose Whittington? I focused on the road and numbness overtook me.

I couldn't find a parking place close to my house, so I parked two streets over. Exhausted, I opened my red lacquered door with the Nantucket silver doorknob and turned on the lights.

My living room was fashioned after Whittington—pale yellow damask wing chairs, the requisite tea table with silver candlesticks, the Persian rugs. My two deviations, contemporary art and my dollhouse. Brushing by the colorful Joan Miró and Jim Dine lithographs, I headed to the kitchen to pour a big glass of wine. There were definite advantages to living alone. No one to cook for or clean up after. No one to belittle me. No disagreements over buying clothes or furniture. I stared at the painting of *Café de la Paix* by Ezra Katz wishing I were in Paris, wishing I were anywhere but in the middle of this crisis.

I went over to my dollhouse. I had built it myself: a scale model—one inch to one foot—of Hill Top, the oldest structure on the campus of Mary Baldwin College. The outside of this Greek revival 48" by 24" by 26" structure was painted cream like all the buildings on campus. I had put sand in the cream paint to resemble the stucco in the life size Hill Top. I remembered then that Johannes Vermeer had put sand in his paint to create texture in the renderings of his hometown of Delft. The living room in my dollhouse was an exact replica, Lilliputian size, of the front hall of Whittington, down to the tiny Irish side table, the pair of fine china vases on the mantle, and the three-point-size sheet music on the grand piano. Only other miniaturists understood its hold over devotees. The change in scale, as in art, fascinated me. More than that, it was a world of my own making that I could totally control.

7

Georgetown

If in doubt, call the psychic. Was that going to be my new M.O.? I sat down with my hot coffee at the kitchen island and punched in Diane's number. She answered on the first ring.

"Hi, Millicent. Hold on. Let me turn this recorder on. What's on your mind?"

I told Diane the entire miserable situation concerning the painting and Lee, her staggering tax bill, the lawsuit. In the ten minutes it took to tell her I was totally drained.

"As I mentioned, Saturn is squaring Uranus in your birth chart," she said. "Saturn is the hard lesson planet. The people who will help you solve your lesson will come into your life."

"So I'm supposed to just sit back and relax?"

"No. You are supposed to follow the signals you receive when you are perfectly still. That's why it is so important to meditate and pray. It's the only time God can get through to us."

"I mean, really, does God involve himself in human affairs?" my voice was loud.

"Yes, he does," Diane said. "He is the living God. But He doesn't interfere with nature. The physical laws operate unimpeded: tsunamis, hurricanes, earthquakes, tornados. I can't explain the universe, but I can tell you, God moves in our lives when we let Him. Our knowledge is limited and always will be. It wasn't that long ago that people thought the sun revolved around the earth. They were convinced of it, because they saw it with their own eyes. The spiritual world is on a much higher plane than the physical world but humankind is not ready to believe it. I'm sure you've heard this before but it bears repeating: we think we are physical beings having spiritual experiences. In truth, we are spiritual beings having physical experiences."

"But what is going to happen to Lee? How is she going to get out of her dilemma? I feel terrible because I caused all of this."

"No, you did not cause it. You are an actor in the play. You will work through this. You have what you need to fulfill your destiny. Don't worry."

Easy for her to say. I wasn't going to solve anything on that front, so I decided to distract myself with questions about my love life, what there was of it. "Well, on another note. The man I've been dating is attractive, successful, I think he loves me, but I'm doing all the work in the relationship."

"When are you going to stop attracting emotionally unavailable men like your father?" Diane's words hit me hard.

"My father… He was wonderful! He would do anything for me!" Daddy had been dead for five years. I fiercely wanted to preserve his memory unblemished.

"Yes, your father was wonderful, but he was emotionally unavailable—as were most dads of his era. Until you separate yourself from your parental imprinting and look to yourself as a whole being, you will keep pulling in men who are not available for an intimate relationship."

"But those are the ones I fall in love with."

"You do that because you want the relationship to have a different ending, but it never will. You will fall in love with the right man when you decide to have a real relationship."

"But I've always wanted a real relationship!"

"You thought you did. What you really wanted was a relationship in which you kept your independence."

"What's wrong with that? All women deserve to be independent."

"It's an issue of commitment," Diane explained. "Being with a man who is remote and unavailable leaves you an out. You don't have to commit because he never will. That's one reason women have relationships with married men. They're safe."

Her words left me completely agitated. Agitated because I was afraid that Diane was right. "So you're saying Phillip is not the one?"

"No, he is not your destiny. He's a place holder."

I let out a big sigh. "Am I never going to find true love?"

"Jupiter conjuncts Venus in your house of marriage early next year," Diane added. "You are going to meet your soul mate soon. The relationship isn't quite ready to unfold. Your first priority is to resolve the challenge in your career path. Something big. You will be called on to use every ability and talent you have. You might already know this, Millicent, but one of your talents is that you are psychic yourself."

"Me?" I protested, taken off guard.

"Your psychic ability can be developed. You have to spend time in solitude, becoming very still, then you can begin to receive images and impressions. Sometimes psychic information comes in dreams or other alpha states."

I thought immediately of the dream I had had at Whittington but rather than mention it, I told Diane I had to go. I held my hand on the phone receiver after I had hung up. Maybe my mother was right. This astrology psychic stuff was a bunch of bunk.

Green Gallery right off Wisconsin Avenue was in the toniest part of Georgetown. I pressed the brass doorbell and waited to be buzzed into the elegant art space. An attractive young woman approached wearing a fitted black outfit with bold jewelry and red lipstick that matched her stilettos.

"Hello. I'm Millicent Clermont. I am here to speak with Richard Green."

"I'm terribly sorry," the young female with a British accent said. "He is not here at the moment. May I give him a message?"

"I need to talk with him. Immediately. I'm a friend of Lee Trevor from Whittington plantation."

Her heavily made-up eyes widened.

"It's regarding the Dutch painting," I told her.

"Mr. Green is really quite ill."

"Please tell me where he is. I've got to get Mrs. Trevor's painting to the National Gallery to be examined."

"Mr. Green is at Sibley Hospital," the art gallery assistant said in a monotone as her shoulders dropped. "I'll go call him and tell him you're coming."

I watched her as she walked her model's walk. Her outfit was beautiful, but the white label showing through her pricey sheer blouse ruined her outfit. Why did designers put unsightly labels on their high dollar blouses? And why didn't the women who wore them cut the labels out? That's the first thing I did, either because the label showed or it was uncomfortable. Consequently part of my wardrobe appeared to come from discount houses rather than off the racks of Neiman-Marcus and Saks, bought on sale of course.

Located in northwest Washington, Sibley Hospital was the society hospital. Andrew Barlow wouldn't be caught dead in any other.

"What room is Richard Green in, please?" I asked the woman at the information desk.

She checked her list. "I'm sorry but that patient is on a protected floor."

"But I'm a good friend."

"Sorry," she gave me that impatient mother look, "He is under police protection."

I silently cursed and turned around to use my cell phone.

"Green Gallery." The English voice answered.

"Hi, this is Millicent Clermont. I'm at Sibley. I can't get into to see Richard."

"Could you hand your cell phone to the receptionist?"

Five minutes later I was riding up the elevator. Two uniformed men guarded Richard Green's room. One of them nodded me in.

Richard looked noticeably thinner and paler from when I had seen him at the Gallery a couple of weeks ago. He adjusted his hospital gown with the words 'Property of Sibley Hospital' as if anyone would steal such an ugly thing.

"Richard, I'm Millicent Clermont, Lee Trevor's friend."

His voice was tired and raspy. "Yes, Millicent. How you are?"

"The question is, how are you?" I asked softly, feeling guilty I had mistrusted this person.

"As bad as I feel, apparently I'll live. This kind of poison only makes one want to die."

"You've been poisoned?" I was aghast.

"The old-fashioned way....arsenic."

I swallowed. "Arsenic? The stuff of murder mysteries? Who is trying to kill you?"

Richard rolled his bloodshot eyes. "I have no idea. I got sick after eating a box of chocolates that were sent to my gallery. I love the wicked candy so I popped away. Then I felt like a slug having salt poured on me."

"I am so sorry, Richard. The only arsenic poisoning I ever heard of was in the movie with Cary Grant, *Arsenic and Old Lace*."

"Fiction and reality, arsenic poisoning is quite prevalent." Richard took a drink of water from the Styrofoam cup on his hospital tray. "Napoleon got it from wallpaper glue. Paint peeling off the walls gave it to Clare Booth Luce. Van Gogh and Monet got sick from the Emerald Green paint pigment they used." Richard's short dissertation had exhausted him. He closed his eyes.

I waited a minute but then told him why I had come. "I really hate to bother you now, but I need to get Lee's painting. Lee and I have been sued over it. The director at the National Gallery has also been sued and wants me to bring it to the Gallery as soon as possible."

Richard opened his eyes in alarm.

"An art dealer in New York bought it."

My jaw dropped. "You sold it?"

"Lee was anxious to move it. I haven't told her yet."

"Did you know it had been stolen by the Nazis?"

"No," Richard murmured. "But few works of art have perfect provenances."

"Do you think it's a real Vermeer?"

Richard weakly held his hands up in the dim hospital room. "The dealer I bought it from didn't know. Happens all the time." Richard closed his eyes again and said in a whisper, "Pet Wilde bought it. Wilde Fine Art on Madison."

"Pet?"

"Short for Petrides. I'm sorry. I'm fading."

"Yes, I need to leave you alone. I hope you feel better."

"Thanks," he said faintly, his eyelids still closed.

8

Manhattan

Before my appointment with Pet Wilde of Wilde Fine Arts on Madison Avenue, I planned to meet my best friend at the Metropolitan Museum of Art. Not only would I not miss a chance to visit my dear friend, I needed a pressure reducer before my meeting with Mr. Wilde. I stepped out of the cab at East 82th Street. Gabby Chapman, the spitting image of Diane Keaton in *Baby Boom,* was waiting for me.

"Millie!"

"Gabby!" Our voices too high. I could smell her signature Prada perfume. "I love your shoes," my eyes drawn to her expensive flats. "Jimmy Choo?"

My patrician-looking friend nodded as we made our way down to the Costume Institute in the lower level to see the Coco Chanel exhibit.

"Coco's given name was Gabrielle too. She changed it to 'Coco' based on a song she sang in Paris bistros."

"Maybe I should go by Coco," my friend mused.

Once inside the exhibit space, we read the exhibition board.

"Wow, she had a lot of lovers," Gabby said as she scanned the print.

"That's where she got some of her ideas— her lovers' closets, it says here," I added.

"Coco had a German lover who was a Nazi spy, thirteen years her junior, a baby-head!" Gabby summarized. "Unusual name. Hans Gunther von Dincklage. Maybe that was the attraction."

"Very funny. Anyway, she must have had some power over Hans—she lived at the Paris Ritz during the German occupation. Her atelier was right across the street from the hotel's back entrance and the Hemingway Bar."

"Yeah, the last door Princess Di walked through before her fatal accident," Gabby said with a grimace.

We turned our gaze on the dimly lighted costumes. The light was so low to preserve the fragile fabric, it took a moment before our eyes adjusted. Then we were dazzled. Coco Chanel's creations had freed women of corsets and feathers. She had created a fashionable uniform for the professional woman, the classic knits that offered complete freedom of movement, before women had broken the glass ceiling in law and business. Could I respect Coco Chanel as much for her creativity knowing that she had cavorted with Nazis? Then I thought of my friends, including my mother and Lee Trevor, whose views I did not share in some areas. I decided to pack this issue away for future consideration.

The exhibit's visual eye candy began to lower my blood pressure. I needed to be calm at my meeting with Pet Wilde this afternoon. I had to leave with Lee's painting.

We left for my friend's apartment on Fifth Avenue at East 63rd, the only good thing that came from her divorce—a rent-controlled flat at a great address.

When we were both engaged to our future ex-husbands, Gabby and I had met at Café Pacific in Dallas. We became instant friends. Gabby's grandfather had been a doctor in East Texas and a member of the Texas legislature. Her parents had led a quieter life. How many times had I heard the story of Gabby's mother telling her "You don't need that" as Gabby admired a cashmere sweater. Ignoring her mother's admonition, Gabby later bought the luxurious knit with her babysitting money.

Gabby carried a tray with hot tea to the living room where we sat on opposite ends of her white custom sofa.

"I went to that psychic you told me about." I accepted the beautiful Royal Crown Derby cup with the hot liquid.

"How was it?" Gabby asked.

"Very interesting. Very."

"Anything you can share?"

"Sure. You know me. An open book. Well, for starters I used to be a French soldier in a past life."

"No-o," Gabby said.

"That's why I love everything French."

"I thought your father *was* part French."

"He was, but not that much," I explained. "He didn't speak French."

"Millie, your name is French, for heaven's sake."

"I know. It means 'to see clearly from a mountain.'"

"What else?" Gabby looked at me expectedly.

"The psychic knew about Whittington. She said it was so important to me because it represents roots and security. And I feared being abandoned."

"Diane told me the same thing. The abandonment part. But she told me that most human beings have a fear of being left alone, either when they are young or at the end of their lives."

"That's a comforting thought."

"We're not supposed to live in fear, Millie. That's the point."

My friend refilled our cups.

"Merci. Anyway, I do find the concept of reincarnation intriguing. It helps make sense of life's inequities. Why do babies starve in Haiti and then die after a short tragic life while my ex-husband and his parents were born into a life of vast wealth thinking they did something to deserve it?"

"I suppose you want to give away all you own and become the next Mother Teresa?" Gabby teased.

"No, you know I don't. But I can't seem to forgive Turny or his parents for the way they treated me." I still got furious when I thought of my ex-husband, John Turner Phillips IV, nicknamed Turny for his love of golf.

He believed his family's money was his ticket to do anything he wanted to do, whenever, with whomever. "I let it happen. That's what makes me so bloody mad!"

"Millie, you ought to write a book. My favorite story from your disastrous marriage was when Turny told you to clean up the house and then left for the weekend to play golf. I wish I had seen his face when he saw all those white paper gloves you stuck around the house. What did you write on them?"

"Passed the white glove test."

"That was pure class. He was such a loser-pants."

"I was so blind to his infidelity." I shook my head. "I suspected he was cheating but buried the truth with layers of daily activities. After he gave me crabs from sleeping around, he had the gall to take one of the bottles of cure I had picked up from *my* doctor and go spend the night with his lover. Later I gave him a brass crab from Virginia Metal Crafters. What a f-ing asshole!"

"What did your friend Luci say about him? That he had more nerve than an abscessed tooth?"

"Really! He even showed me the monogrammed boxer shorts his lover had given him." I was spitting my words.

"I hadn't heard that one. Did you hit him?" Gabby leaned forward.

"Oh, no, I was *so* nice. Talk about designer doormat! I pointed to his initials on the front flap of the underwear and told him: 'I guess that's what she likes best about you.'" I emptied my cup in one swallow and let out a loud sigh. "How can we be incredibly smart as professionals and so unbelievably dumb when it comes to our marriages?"

"We should start our own *First Wives' Club*. I'll play Diane Keaton," Gabby pronounced. My best friend looked and acted so much like the funny actress it was uncanny.

"She's your twin for sure. I'll play Bette Midler," I said.

"No, you remind me exactly of Julia Louis-Dreyfus, same personality."

"Thank you. I like that comparison."

"Changing the subject, how's your new love interest?"

I frowned. "Phillip's a bit distant."

"We always love the ones who are hard to get. No hover-crafts for us. You'd think we were men," Gabby said.

"We were. We were French soldiers in the eighteenth century. I'm sure of it."

Gabby got up and looked out her window onto Central Park. "I miss Titus."

Titus Winston had been our octogenarian friend who had lived in the penthouse of Gabby's building. His apartment was part library and part Asian museum. Books were stacked next to upholstered chairs, stacked on every table, sharing space with Thai sculpture, overlapping Persian rugs, and an impressive collection of boxes, large and small, antique and new, neatly arranged on mirrored tables. "Boxes are most interesting," Titus would say. "You have one idea of who they are from the outside and another idea after you open them. Like people." Or, "Tools seek to be used," he would start, ruminating on the manufacture of guns or garden tools. And his famous discussion on 'verticality' and other concepts of human evolution was always a full bottle visit. Gabby and I had spent hours listening to him. Titus had died in his sleep a year ago. We had attended his service at the United Nations.

"I miss him, too, but he had a full life," I said, joining Gabby at the window.

"I hate when people say that. Don't say that about me." Gabby's face was serious.

"Do you think our loved ones know how much we loved them?" I asked. "Do our thoughts about them attach to their soul?" We watched people walking down Fifth Avenue, some walking fast, some slow. "That's the concept Carlos Ruiz Zafón created in his book, *The Shadow of the Wind*, except instead of thoughts becoming part of a person's soul, whoever reads a particular book becomes part of that book's soul."

"That's something to consider," Gabby nodded, still focused outside.

"I think that could apply to paintings as well," I added. "Everyone who gazes at a painting becomes part of that painting's soul. Sort of disgusting when you think of paintings the Nazis stole. Remember how we met Titus?"

"Of course. You started talking to a stranger, a distinguished stranger, but still a stranger, sitting next to us at Le Relais and the next thing I know we're on his rooftop terrace looking out over Central Park as we're doing right now."

Gabby and I had gone to dinner at our favorite French restaurant on Madison right around the corner. We were seated at the long banquette against the far wall. We couldn't decide what to order so I had asked the elegantly dressed, silver-haired man with a beard to my right, "Is that good?" referring to his steak and frits. He had smiled graciously. I couldn't avoid noticing his large gold ring in the shape of a lion's head. "My, that ring must have quite a story," I had said. Titus had taken his heavy ring off and handed it to me to inspect. That had started a friendship among the three of us that lasted until his death.

"We better get going. My appointment is at two."

"There's a new restaurant where Le Relais used to be. Let's go to lunch there," Gabby suggested.

"Perfect. The Wilde gallery is just up the street."

After lunch, I hugged Gabby goodbye and headed north on Madison. Wilde Fine Arts announced its presence with your typical high-end polished brass and glass entrance through which expensive framed art with perfect lighting sent the unmistakable message: don't enter unless you have money, lots of it. I opened the heavy door and was greeted immediately by a well-dressed good-looking young man, his black hair slicked back and glossy.

"May I help you?" he asked in a practiced voice, his eyebrows arched.

"Yes. Pet Wilde is expecting me. Millicent Clermont from the National Gallery."

"One moment please." He turned in his polished shoes toward the back.

I looked around the gallery. Quite a collection. Old Masters. Impressionists.

Pet Wilde walked out energetically, extending his hand from his impeccable suit, white collared striped shirt, gold cufflinks. "Millicent. Welcome to Wilde Fine Arts." His silver hair was coiffed.

"Thank you," I said, a bit taken back with his exuberance.

"May we offer you a beverage? A glass of wine? Perrier?" he continued his surprising hospitality.

"Perrier would be great. Thanks."

"Antonio? Would you mind?" He turned to the young man who had first greeted me. Antonio nodded once and returned to the rear of the gallery.

"Please have a seat," the gallery owner said, motioning me to a coral velvet chair. "What can I do for you today?"

"As you know Richard Green is in the hospital."

"Yes. We were sorry to hear he had taken ill," Pet said with a slight frown.

"Apparently Richard will recover. Eventually. But I am here to discuss the painting he sent from Whittington plantation. A Dutch painting." I couldn't believe I sounded so professional, so clinical, about Lee's favorite painting.

"Let me think. Dutch painting.... he sold me several," Pet said with a wave of his hand as he seemed to scan his memory bank. He instantly reminded me of other 'Don't Ask, Don't Tell' secretive art dealers.

Antonio came back with the Perrier.

"It looks like a Vermeer," I said, giving him a clue he didn't need.

"Oh, I do think I remember that one. A small canvas. Not particularly well executed to the trained eye. Some might say it's in the school of Vermeer. Certainly Dutch."

Anger lit my veins. But an inner voice said: stay calm, play the game, if you show your cards, it's over. "That's the one," I said in a monotone. "John Peale sent me to ask you if we might exhibit it in our next show on Dutch artists."

"The National Gallery of Art is doing an exhibition on Dutch painters? I hadn't read about it."

"It's in the planning stages," I answered quickly, recovering from my on-the-spot lie. "We can't very well announce an exhibit before we have the most significant pieces loaned," I finished with a grin more at my own cleverness than at the gallery owner. "But we need it as soon as possible. I was hoping I could pick it up while I'm here."

Pet Wilde narrowed his eyes for a second then grinned tightly. "Well, in that case we wouldn't want to pass up this opportunity. The problem is my sister-in-law currently has the painting. It's not here."

Another dead end. Pushing down my frustration, I coolly said, "I'll be happy to collect it from her. Give me her address and I'll be out of your hair." *Your frozen gray hair.*

His eyes darted around the room. "Let me call her. I'll be right back."

After Pet was out of sight, I sank in the coral chair and scanned the gallery again. Chagall, Monet, Pissarro, Rembrandt and Turner. Millions of dollars of art stared back at me. Several minutes went by. I put my glass down and glanced at my watch. 2:30 p.m. If I could get Lee's painting soon, I could still make the shuttle back to D.C. tonight.

Pet returned considerably less energetic. "Luck has it I caught my sister-in-law before she was leaving. She's on the northwest corner of 34th and Lexington. Warner House, number 204. Millicent, it's been a pleasure. I've got another appointment. Here's my card. Give my regards to the director."

I put the stiff oversized business card in my purse. "You didn't tell me your sister-in-law's name."

"Mrs. Baader," Pet Wilde said in a grave tone, looking different from the person I had been talking with.

9

Manhattan

Mrs. Baader's apartment building on 34th and Lexington wasn't the luxury home I had expected for the sister-in-law of one of the most venerable art dealers in New York. I looked in disgust at the dented and dirty metal mailbox with handwritten names and pushed the button for number 204.

"Ja?" A voice with a heavy German accent blared.

"Mrs. Baader? It's Millicent Clermont. Pet Wilde arranged my visit."

"Ein moment."

A loud buzzer let me in. As I climbed up the grimy steps to the second landing, a slight odor of urine engulfed me. A heavyset woman with a full head of hair stood in an open doorway. How could Pet Wilde be so stylish and his sister-in-law completely the opposite? She motioned me in. Her home was military clean, neat as a pin. The only things of beauty were several small paintings stacked against the walls. One photo leaned on the austere mantel. The door locked behind me with a noisy click, making me jump slightly.

"Pet told me you wanted painting," Mrs. Baader said in a strange voice. "Come take look." She could have used etiquette lessons from Lee Trevor, although the idea of the two of them in the same room was inconceivable. She motioned me to the paintings on the bare floor.

"Thank you, Mrs. Baader. I'm sure it won't take long." I went over to one of the stacks, knelt down, and carefully flipped through the framed canvases. Not one artist did I recognize. On the other hand, if she owned any well-known artist, I couldn't imagine why she lived here. Why wouldn't she hang some of the paintings? The world was full of totally weird people and half of them lived in New York City. And here I was alone in one of the crazies' apartments.

She watched me with such intensity as I looked through the paintings, it made my skin crawl. "Hurry up. I don't have all day." The old woman's demeanor was cross.

"These are nice pieces, Mrs. Baader. Where did you acquire them?" I asked, trying to lighten the oppressive mood in the room.

"I brought them with me when I moved to New York, Fraulein. After my husband died."

"Oh, I'm so sorry. Is that a picture of him?" indicating the frame on the fake mantel. I stood up and started to walk over to take a closer look, doing what development officers did to establish rapport with prospective donors.

"Do not bring up past." Her rough voice startled me. "You are here to find painting."

"Of course." I retreated quickly. The light from the window fell on Mrs. Baader's face. You'd think at her age she would have given up wearing so much makeup. I kneeled down and resumed gingerly flipping through one of the stacks. How she could be married to Pet's brother was a mystery. I moved to another stack of paintings on the floor.

"All of these are beautiful, Mrs. Baader." I was at a lost as what to say. Mrs. Baader obviously didn't want to talk. I was now going through the third stack of oils. Still no sign of Lee's painting. I could hear Mrs. Baader's heavy breathing. She probably snored like a freight train. I glanced up and happened to look into the adjoining bedroom.

And then I saw it. "There it is. The small painting of the woman in blue. That's it!" I announced.

"Not for sale," Mrs. Baader's face was hard.

"Well, actually, Mrs. Baader, I'm not here to buy it. Officially it still belongs to Mrs. Trevor in Virginia. I'm here to take it to the National Gallery of Art. Didn't Pet tell you?" My firmness surprised me.

Mrs. Baader eyed me in a bizarre way. "I have many paintings. That one not for sale."

My stomach registered panic. "Mrs. Baader," I repeated as I walked toward the bedroom where Lee's painting was propped against a chair, "I came to get this painting."

Mrs. Baader grabbed me roughly by the arm. "Stop now."

"Ouch." I retrieved my arm and looked into Mrs. Baader's cold gray eyes.

"I told you," she said menacing. "Not for sale. Come sit." Her voice suddenly lightened. "We talk."

I was supposed to carry on a conversation with a German woman who spoke English in two word sentences? Not knowing what else to do, I slowly followed the chunky woman with the heavy step over to the plain table. On the way, she jerked the thin curtain closed to block the sun. The only object on the table was a stark white plate with dark brown chocolates.

"Sit. Have chocolate. Special from Belgium."

I sat on the farthest chair from where she lowered herself down with a thump.

"Your brother-in-law did tell you why I came, didn't he, Mrs. Baader?" I felt perspiration penetrate my jacket. And then another surge of panic hit me. Richard was in the hospital from eating chocolate. Had Mrs. Baader sent the poison chocolates to Richard? I looked in horror at the plate of dark squares and pretended to adjust my glasses, trying to think. I quickly wiped the beads of sweat at my hairline and returned my hands to my lap. Maybe I should leave and come back later for the painting. But would it still be here? I sat there frozen in my indecision.

"Have chocolate," she ordered, pushing the plate toward me.

"O-kay," I said mechanically. My mouth was as dry as bone. I slowly picked up a dark brown square, trying to figure out how I was going to avoid eating it. The piece of chocolate felt gooey in my fingers. What if I didn't eat it? Would Mrs. Baader shoot me? Her big rough hands could squeeze the air out my windpipe in seconds. No one except Pet Wilde knew I was here. No one. How was I going to get Lee's painting? Was I going to die here in this ugly apartment?

At that moment, a loud noise made me jump as the front door flew open like an exploding bomb. Four men in black suits stormed into the small living room holding guns. Behind them was none other than Haywood Tabb.

"Millicent, drop that chocolate!" Haywood shouted as he leveled his gun at Mrs. Baader. "It's poison!"

Stunned, the lethal bonbon fell out of my hand as I fell back in my chair. Two of the suited men grabbed Mrs. Baader, dragging her away from the table. In seconds they had her handcuffed.

Haywood held up a shiny silver badge. "Otto Baader," Haywood said, "you are under arrest for transporting stolen art across states lines." He then pulled off Mrs. Baader's wig revealing a short gray crew cut.

Mrs. Baader was a man.

"Once extradited to Washington, D.C.," Haywood pronounced, "you will be charged with the attempted murder of Richard Green." Baader narrowed his eyes but said nothing.

I felt the blood drain from my face as two of the agents led the silent Baader with his short hair and old woman's dress out of the grungy apartment.

Haywood turned to me. "Are you all right, Millicent?"

I looked at Haywood, bewildered. "What's going on? I thought you were a lawyer."

"I am a lawyer," Haywood said as he put his gun away. "I also work undercover for the F.B.I. You have just met the son of a Nazi general. Herr Baader is one of the most wanted art thieves in the world." Haywood walked into the other room and carefully picked up Lee's painting. "I'll help you get this to the National Gallery."

"How did you know I was here?" I asked, still in shock.

"I'll tell you on the way to the Waldorf."

I followed Haywood out. "The Waldorf?"

"I'm giving a speech there tonight and you shouldn't be traveling by yourself back to Washington. We'll take the shuttle back early in the morning."

I was too exhausted to argue, but there was one thing I still wanted to know. "You sue me and my mentor and then save my life? What kind of bi-polar nutcase are you?"

We reached the sidewalk and a black car appeared out of nowhere. F.B.I. limo service. Haywood opened the back door for me. "I didn't sue you, Millicent."

As I stepped into the car, Haywood handed me Lee's

painting, and went around to the other door. I gently placed the Dutch painting in the middle of the seat.

"Well, you told someone about the painting and they filed suit," I said as he sat down. "It was published in an online magazine. The National Gallery is also named in the suit."

"I didn't tell a soul. Have you been served?"

"Not yet. How could you do this? Is this some revenge you're taking out on Whittington?"

"Whoa, pony. That's not what I'm about at all."

"Then tell me who has ruined my life and Lee's, and created a P.R. nightmare for the Gallery. You've got to have some idea, Mr. F.B.I."

"At the moment, I don't. But I can find out who the plaintiffs are and who their legal counsel is."

"Lawyers!" I said, disgusted.

"But you are one."

"Yeah, the best kind. Non-practicing," I barked.

I stared out the window as the car made its way uptown, the last hour's events spinning in my head. I turned to Haywood. "So, why did Otto Baader dress in women's clothing?"

"Apparently after Otto's wife died, he began wearing her clothes. Not only to distance himself from his high-ranking Nazi father, but also to avoid detection and prosecution for his art crimes. We suspect he was involved in the Isabella Gardner Museum heist. What we don't know is why Baader poisoned Richard Green and tried to poison you."

"Could there be poison on my hand?" I turned my hand over in horror.

"I doubt it. And it would be such a small amount, it couldn't kill you."

I pulled a Wet One from my purse and wiped my hands. Who would have thought fundraising for the arts could be so dangerous?

"What is Baader's connection to Pet Wilde?"

"Otto Baader is Pet Wilde's half brother. Pet Wilde presents himself as the respectable branch of the family. So far Wilde has been able to escape prosecution although he's been sued in the past for dealing in Nazi stolen art. We believe he's as guilty as his brother, only slicker."

"Pet is slicker for sure. I never would have guessed they shared any DNA."

"Otto is General Wilhelm Baader's son by his German wife. Petrides is his son by his Parisian mistress, Marie Wilde, whose name Pet took. We're hoping Baader will divulge information about his brother to save his own skin."

"When did you start working for the F.B.I., Haywood?"

"I went in right after law school. Have you ever heard of the 333rd Field Artillery Battalion?"

"No." I shook my head.

"It was a World War II all-black battalion," Haywood explained. "In 1944 near the Belgium village of Wereth, eleven soldiers from the 333rd were found with broken legs and arms, cut off fingers, bayonet wounds to their faces, their bodies obviously tortured. They were called the 'Wereth 11.' My uncle was one of them."

"I am sorry. That is horrible."

"The SS troops who did it were never prosecuted," Haywood said heatedly. "My calling is returning artwork stolen by the Nazis. My passion is finding criminals with Nazi connections."

We stopped at 50th and Park Avenue. The Waldorf bellman opened the car door and we entered the grand entrance of the historic hotel. Haywood and I went straight to the hotel manager and watched as Lee's painting was put in a security vault.

Then every ounce of energy drained out of me. "I need to crash," I told Haywood. "I'll see you in the morning." Good thing I carried a little make up in my purse so I wouldn't look completely unpresentable tomorrow. I wish I could have called Gabby but she was flying out of New York after our lunch today. Was that today?

"Get a good night's sleep. You're safe here. F.B.I. agents are staying on your floor."

As furious as I had been at Haywood, I was relieved he was accompanying me to Washington. My once independent and brave spirit was waning. I felt vulnerable. As odd and frightening as Mrs. Baader was, I was shocked she turned out to be a he. The world was not the benign place I trusted it was. Obvious monsters were terrifying enough. That beautiful devil, Pet Wilde, chilled me to the bone.

Part Two

"There is no trusting appearances."
Richard Sheridan

10

Manhattan
Washington, D.C.

The Waldorf=Astoria was the first hotel to allow women to enter without escorts and to offer room service. The double hyphen was added when Hilton Corporation bought it. "Meet me at the hyphen" became a well-worn phrase. My room, a Junior League special offered at considerably lower rates, was the size of a shoebox. I had dressed and eaten my last bite of breakfast when the phone rang.

"Millicent, good morning. It's Haywood. I have something important to show you."

"Sure. I'm in room …"

"We know where you are. Be right there."

When I opened my door, Haywood stood there holding a black portfolio.

"Let me show you how this works." With a gleeful expression, Haywood laid the portfolio on the bed. "See this little device under the concealed compartment?"

I saw a small knob the size of my thumb.

"Wherever this goes, the F.B.I. knows."

"A tracking device like in the movies?" I asked.

"Bingo. It's on a Global Positioning System connected directly to the Federal Bureau of Investigation," Haywood said with great satisfaction. "If someone were to take the painting, we could trace it immediately."

"Is this really necessary?" I screwed up my face.

"Baader was willing to kill for the painting. If Pet Wilde is involved, and we believe he is, he's clever enough to get someone else to do his dirty work."

We took the elevator to the first floor and retrieved Lee's painting from the hotel safe.

Haywood put it into the portfolio and zipped it. We walked out the Park Avenue entrance and took a taxi to LaGuardia Airport.

Haywood handed me the portfolio with its special tracer and important cargo as we entered the Gallery's East Building. Thankfully this early it was free of crowds.

"I'm going to run to the men's room. I'll be right back," Haywood said.

I waited under the huge Miró tapestry. Now that I was delivering the painting to the director, I could relax. At least about that. I had called the director's assistant telling her I had Lee's painting. John Peale would be waiting for us in his office.

A hard bump from behind jolted me. A rough hand

grabbed the portfolio. I turned to see a disheveled man in dirty clothes.

"Wait! You can't have that!" I yelled as the man took off toward the museum entrance, his stringy hair and soiled jacket flapping above the shiny black case.

I spotted Thomas, the security guard. "Thomas, grab the portfolio!" I waved my hands.

Thomas kicked the thief, tearing the man's hand from the handles. The thief managed to regain his balance and ran out the door as other guards followed him.

"Got it," Thomas said, holding up the black rectangle.

"Thank God, Thomas. Thank you so much." My heart was pumping out of my chest. My hands shook as I took the portfolio. Was that an accident or a set-up by the F.B.I. to test their toy? Where was Haywood?

Haywood came calmly out of the men's room and walked over adjusting his tie.

"A man tried to steal the painting," I exclaimed.

"Was he caught?" Haywood looked around.

"He ran out the door, Mr. Tabb. Our security men went after him," Thomas said.

"I'll be right back." Haywood sprinted toward the entrance.

"Thomas, would you go with me to the director's office please?"

"Sure, Miss Millicent. Glad to."

Once we were behind the glass doors marked Administrative Offices, I exhaled and walked over to the elevator banks. Lee's painting had lived peacefully for fifty years at Whittington. The last twenty-four hours were out of a Stephen King movie. Thomas and I approached the director's office. The Gallery's Vermeer expert, Paul Morton, was talking to John Peale when we walked in. I told them what had happened downstairs.

"Good work, Thomas," the director said.

"Yes, sir. Just doing my job." Thomas tipped his hat and left.

John Peale and Paul Morton couldn't wait to see the three hundred and fifty year old painting. I unzipped the portfolio and gently placed Lee's painting on the director's table.

"This is an intriguing piece," John said, nodding. "Paul, what do you think?"

Paul Morton removed his horn-rimmed glasses and bent over the painting. "It certainly is in the school of Vermeer. Of course, we'll have to verify that this painting is the same one on the list of Nazi looted art. Artists often paint the same scene but with minor variations."

"Paul, what exactly do you do to authenticate a painting?" I asked.

"We look at the materials the artists used: the type and age of the paint, the canvas or board used," the Harvard-educated curator explained. "We take minute samples of paint and put them under a microscope to identify the pigment. We also look at the underdrawings, brushstrokes, and other identifying aspects through

X-rays, infrared photographs and reflectograms. Those are some of the things we do."

"That's fascinating. How long will it take until we know the results?" I asked, hoping I didn't sound too anxious. "Mrs. Trevor needs this resolved quickly."

"A couple of weeks," Paul said. "Depends what else is going on in Conservation."

"It will be the longest couple of weeks in my life."

"We're all in this together, Millicent," John said.

I wished I believed him.

Haywood entered the director's office.

"Did you find out who tried to steal the painting?" I asked Haywood.

"Apparently, a guy off the street who was promised a hundred dollar bill if he could snatch it. He couldn't describe his future benefactor except to say he was fat with glasses and his suit was rumpled."

I left the Gallery without going by my office. I couldn't wait to climb into my own bed in my own home. I opened my front door and froze. My house was in complete shambles, tables turned over, cushions off the sofa and chairs, total chaos. I ran next door and knocked hard on Andrew's door.

"Andrew! Andrew! Are you there?"

Andrew opened his door. "Millicent. What's wrong?"

"Someone has broken into my house!"

He closed his door and followed me.

"What a mess." Andrew shook his head as he looked around my torn up townhouse. I called the D.C. police.

Once the police officers arrived, they checked the doors and windows for entry marks as I counted my silver flatware and other valuables in the living room and kitchen.

"Not a typical break-in," Officer Dancer said. "Anything stolen?"

"I can't tell that anything is missing down here," I replied.

"You want to take us upstairs, Miss Clermont?"

"As long as you go first." Andrew and I followed the officers up the stairs.

My bedroom was a wreck. I went immediately to my jewelry box. The Barry Kieselstein-Cord falcon I had bought after my divorce as a symbol of my freedom was the most expensive piece I owned. It was right there. My entire townhouse was a disaster, but nothing appeared to be missing. I was grateful for that. But the thought of someone rifling through my personal things made me cringe. I called Haywood.

"I'll be right over," he said and hung up.

Haywood carefully examined my entire house as Andrew and I put the living room back in place. Haywood came down the stairs. "A clean job. Means whoever broke in is a professional. He picked the lock on your backdoor like a locksmith."

"I don't know if that's better or worse," I looked from Haywood to Andrew.

"The burglar was looking for something specific," Haywood said. "Something interrupted him and he fled or he couldn't find what he was looking for."

"Could this be related to what happened at the Gallery an hour ago?" I asked, feeling my emotions coming to the surface.

Haywood placed his hand on my shoulder. "Could be. Are you all right?"

At the sight of his concern, I broke down.

"We'll get coverage on your place immediately," Haywood said as he pulled out his cell phone. "They'll be here in a matter of minutes."

"Millicent, I'll stay until they arrive." Andrew handed me his handkerchief.

I nodded thanks.

"Don't hesitate to call me," Haywood added, closing the front door behind him.

I composed myself and gave Andrew his handkerchief. "You don't have to stay. I'll be all right. I need to get some rest."

"Are you sure?"

I nodded.

"You know where I am. Take care, dah-ling. Lock the door behind me."

I followed Andrew to the door and turned the dead bolt once he had left. I dragged myself up to my bedroom and pulled the bedspread back on the bed, too tired to change the sheets. Just as sleep was taking me, the doorbell rang. Haywood must have forgotten something. Or maybe it was Andrew. I plodded downstairs. I peered through the peephole. It wasn't Haywood or Andrew. I opened the door an inch.

A process server handed me an envelope showing the return address of a New York law firm. "Please sign here," he directed. I slammed the door and ripped open the envelope. My hands shook as I read.

UNITED STATES DISTRICT COURT FOR THE
DISTRICT OF COLUMBIA

Colette Alexander and Jacques Alexander,
Plaintiffs/Appellants
vs.
Lee Trevor, Millicent Clermont, John Peale and
the National Gallery of Art,
Defendants/Appellees.

As many times as I have seen petitions, even written them, seeing my name and Lee's in black and white as defendants sent electrical fear through my veins. Seeing my boss' name and the National Gallery electrocuted me again. Of course they were asking for the return of the painting. They also were demanding court costs and $100,000 in damages. Besides the money, what if this cost me my job? What if it cost me my mentor Lee Trevor?

11

Lake Aluma
Oklahoma

Desperate for a break, I took Friday off and flew to Oklahoma City. I needed to get out of D.C. I needed to visit my mother.

For a long time I was an East Coast snob and hated going to Oklahoma. After Daddy died, I felt differently. Maybe it was my guilt. All those things I wished I had done. The letters I could have written. The trips to see him I could have made.

In the meantime, Oklahoma City had transformed itself. The historic Skirvin Hotel had reopened. The Museum of Art had moved to the renovated old theater downtown. Devon Energy had built the impressive fifty-story Devon Tower. Chesapeake Arena, named after Oklahoma City's other big energy company, was the new home of the NBA Oklahoma City Thunder.

I landed at Will Rogers World Airport and took the escalator to baggage claim. The word 'world' in the name always struck me as amusing. 'World via mucho connections' was more accurate. I pulled my bag from the carousel and noticed the handle smashed and the frame dented. I prayed my new six hundred dollar high heels, not yet paid for, had survived. An underworked bag handler happy to make a tip took my now dented luggage to American Airlines baggage claim.

I would have carried my bag on board and saved the fifty dollars if we weren't restricted to three ounce bottles, thanks to terrorists. Even though I had my hair gel, hair spray, face toner, and good body lotion in small containers, I needed more than a quart size plastic zip bag.

"You have to wonder what possibly could have caused this sort of damage," I told the agent.

"American Airlines doesn't fix handles," she said as we examined the obliterated handle. "But since it has a major dent to the frame, they might replace it. If anything inside is damaged, we'll need receipts, that sort of thing," the agent explained.

"My shoes inside are brand new. And I usually keep receipts for clothes for ten years."

"You do?"

"I'm kidding. But perhaps I should start."

I exited the airport and grabbed a cab to Lake Aluma, a small town on the outskirts of Oklahoma City.

I opened the back door to my mother's Lake Aluma house and walked through her kitchen into the dining room. Her small Persian rugs were rolled and stacked in a corner.

"Mommy, what are these rugs doing here?" Forty years old and I still could not call her anything else except in public. My mother, Catherine Clermont, was seventy years old but most guessed she was ten years younger. She resembled the model Carmen with her white hair, high cheekbones, and tailored clothing. As far as personality, Shirley MacLaine playing Aurora in *Terms of Endearment* was my mother on the big screen.

"Oh, I don't want to get them dirty," my mother explained as if that made all the sense in the world.

"Isn't that what rugs are for? I worry about all these throw rugs around. You could trip and fall."

"Throw rugs are good because I can wash them," my mother said.

I rolled my eyes and changed the subject.

"Where's Godiva?"

"She's in the back yard."

I walked outside and marveled at the puffy clouds—white peonies in a hyacinth blue sky—and saw my chocolate lab bouncing toward me like a wooden rocking horse. As if on cue, the white egrets in a perfect line on the opposite bank fluttered up and away.

"How's my girl?" I hugged Godiva but she quickly moved out of my reach and stood near the door. It had broken my heart to give her up, but I was gone too much with my new job and Godiva hated being by herself. I had cried and cried, but after all, she was on land and lake and free to roam.

I let us in and she ran straight to my mother. Godiva had already transferred her allegiance. My mother wasn't a dog person, but she had agreed to take Godiva for me. Now Godiva hardly paid any attention to me. I guessed that was how mothers felt when their children left home.

My mother cleared a place on the dining room table, arranging two placemats and silverware. I had talked her into using her sterling every day, another Whittington practice. Lee put her heavy monogrammed flatware in the dishwasher, so of course I did too. We couldn't wear out sterling in our lifetime or the lifetime of any one we knew. So why not use it everyday?

I noticed more papers than usual stacked on various surfaces. A lot of junk mail, some opened with the original envelopes, some unopened. Plastic wrappers and rubber bands from the newspapers.

"What's all this stuff?" I tried not to sound too judgmental.

"Don't touch anything. I have to go through it. I haven't had the energy."

"But some of this junk mail is months old. Just people asking for money." I could hear my voice becoming strained.

"Yes, but I want to look at it. And um, I want to support certain causes."

My mother's habit of adding "and um" to her sentences

was back. Sometimes it even came out "an dum." Take off the judge's robe, I told myself.

"How's your new computer?" I asked, wanting to talk about something else.

"Oh, I haven't been ready to learn the new program. It's so different from the last one."

"I could tell you weren't reading your email. I've sent you dozens of emails and I never got a response. Maybe we can get on your computer later."

I took a bite of her roast beef. My mother was a great cook even though she never used a recipe and would be hard put to duplicate one of her great meals.

"This is delicious. How did you cook it?" I asked.

"I don't really remember. A little olive oil, a little garlic."

"How's your new security system?" I couldn't help myself from going through my mental checklist.

"Great. I feel so much safer. And um, it works for sure. The other day I forgot I had left bread in the toaster. It set off the alarm and the fire truck came out. I heard the phone ring, but I don't know how they expect me to answer the phone and tell them not to come when I am busy putting out the flames. But the firemen were very nice about it."

"Well, at least it's operative," I replied. I had listened to friends lamenting about their parents slowing down and then exhibiting unusual behavior. Letting things accumulate around the house. Taking forever to accomplish household tasks. I told myself not to freak out. I needed to stay focused on the big issues. I debated whether to tell my mother about the lawsuit and Lee's painting. I decided to wait.

"Are you enjoying Godiva being here?

"Yes. Well, it's a lot of work fixing her mush every day."

"Mush?"

"I cook eggs with corn meal. She gobbles it up."

"Mommy, all you have to do is feed her dry dog food. That and a little cheese to get her to mind."

"I'll try that. She might really miss the mush. Anyway, she is a sweet dog. She watches television with me. Really watches. And um, she'll run up and lick the screen when she sees a dog. One time I left the classical music channel on when I left on an errand. When I came back she was sitting right in front of the TV watching the music credits. She took one look at me and then turned back to resume listening to her classical music. It was the funniest thing."

The next morning God rolled his sparkling diamonds across the lake as the silver sun rose above green velvet trees. The smell of coffee drew me into the kitchen.

"I thought we would go shopping ..." my mother said, "and um, come back and rest before getting dressed for the museum reception tonight."

"Sounds good. I'm going to take a walk around the lake with Godiva."

"She'll love that," my mother told me as if I didn't know.

As I watched Godiva stop and sniff, I thought of the things she did to distinguish herself when she was growing up. When she was a rambunctious puppy, she put her paws into a wet cement sidewalk in Georgetown before I could stop her, leaving a lasting impression.

The legs of my four-poster bed still had her teeth marks. At the time I was furious, but now they were reminders of my little furry baby. However, I could have killed her when she ate one of my cashmere lined leather gloves. I yelled at her as she chomped, chomped on the soft sapphire blue leather, the fingers of the glove getting smaller and smaller. The next day I found a disgusting wad of leather and cashmere that had made its way out of her stomach. Oh, dogs. Oh, sweet Godiva.

How I needed this walk. After the first mile, the world began to make sense again. I loved Virginia and Washington D.C., but I had to admit the big skies of Oklahoma gave me psychic space. I passed a large cottonwood. The trees' bright yellow leaves—gold coins on a gypsy skirt—danced with the wind. Everything is going to be all right, everything is going to be all right, I chanted. The breeze ruffled the surface of the lake.

Back at my mother's, I showered, dressed, and then checked out each room. The living room was orderly and stylish. I picked up a photo of my handsome father. Dead at sixty-six. Sudden heart attack. He had worked so hard his entire life—working in a movie theater during high school, putting himself through college on a football scholarship, becoming a pilot in the Air Force. My parents sacrificed to send me to Mary Baldwin College, spending a third of their monthly income on my tuition. If only he had made full colonel. If only he had lived longer. If only, if only.

Then Congress changed the payout of military widows' annuities, a plan my father, not the government, had paid for every year. The unilateral action for which there was no recourse took away eight hundred dollars a month from my mother. Eight hundred dollars a month from a widow living on the annuity my father paid for. Last year they reversed their egregious mistake but not retroactively.

Now I compulsively changed every toilet tissue roll in every bathroom even in restaurants so the flap was on top, per Daddy's orders growing up. Now I ate Daddy's favorite cashews whenever they were served. Now I came to Oklahoma more often.

"Mommy, are you ready?" I walked into my mother's bedroom and bath, which as usual, reminded me of a Kandinsky painting: colorful clothes, papers, glasses, books, and makeup (mostly with the tops off) on every surface in vast disarray. How she could put herself together—a phoenix rising out of the ashes—and walk out the door looking so attractive was a daily miracle.

12

Oklahoma City Museum of Art
Oklahoma City

It took us all of thirteen minutes to drive downtown to the Oklahoma City Museum of Art. We parked on the street in front. There were tradeoffs everywhere; D.C. was exciting but it took divine intervention to get a parking space near one's destination.

Before joining the reception, we took in the museum's colorful hand-blown glass collection—luminous, glorious eye candy by Dale Chihuly.

"You know this museum has the largest Chihuly collection in the world. And um, the artist has only one eye," my mother announced.

A waiter offered us glasses of champagne on a tray.

"Catherine, so good to see you," the museum director approached us with a man I did not know. "Millicent, it's good to have you in town. Let me introduce you to David Perry from California. David, Catherine Clermont and her daughter, Millicent Clermont from Washington, D.C."

"How do you do, Mrs. Clermont. Millicent." The man greeted us with a charismatic face. Tall and good-looking with salt and pepper hair, a cross between Kevin Kline and Clint Eastwood.

"Where in California do you live, Mr. Perry?" my mother asked.

"Call me David. San Diego. I teach art history at the University of California."

"Millicent, do you live in the District?" David's eyes were on me.

"Yes. Georgetown. I raise money for the National Gallery of Art."

"I'm there frequently on business," he peered at me closely.

"Oh," my mother nodded. I could hear her brain working.

"What is your specialty?" I asked the art professor.

"The World War II art market. Art that the Nazis bought or confiscated, both real and fake," he said.

What was this? National Nazi Looted Art Awareness Week? I could hardly believe my ears. "I'm in the middle of a lawsuit over a painting purportedly stolen by the Nazis," I said.

"You are?" My mother looked at me shocked.

"I haven't had a chance to fill you in," I apologized to her. "I took an art restitution lawyer to my mentor's plantation. Haywood Tabb announced that Mrs. Trevor's Dutch painting was on the list of Nazi looted art. "

"I know Haywood well," David nodded. "He is a fine lawyer and a great guy. One of the best around."

Suddenly my high heels wobbled. My mother's eyes were popping out of her carefully made up face. I took another glass of champagne from a passing waiter as the museum director began her presentation. Saved by the bell. After her talk, I handed David my card and said what I say to everyone, "When you're in Washington and want a tour of the Gallery, give me call."

"I might take you up on that. And if I can help in any way with your situation, please feel free to call me." He gave me his card. He beamed his blue eyes into mine for an extra second that sent sensations through my body. Then he turned and I watched him saunter away, his broad shoulders stacked on a nice athletic frame.

"Too bad he lives in California," my mother said as we walked outside.

"What difference does it make where he lives?"

"Well, if he lived closer to Washington, you could get to know him faster."

"Mommy, you don't know if he is married, or anything about him."

"I don't think he is. I just have a feeling. And um, the two of you would make an attractive couple."

"That is the most ridiculous thing I have ever heard. I talked to the man for two seconds."

"That's all it takes."

I shook my head. Lee and I had been sued, her painting might be a stolen Vermeer, and my mother had me matched up with a complete stranger who lived three thousand miles away. Definitely more protein. I was going to need it.

"I've got my hands full dealing with Lee Trevor's painting. Plus, I'm dating someone."

"Who are you dating?" She turned to look at me.

"A writer."

"A writer? What does he write?" my mother quizzed me.

"Fiction. Legal thrillers. He's quite successful."

"Where does he live?" She continued, a dog on a bone.

"Dallas."

"Where did you meet him?"

"At the Gallery."

One of my favorite donors had introduced me to Phillip Gray, the spitting image of Richard Gere. Dressed in a cream-colored leather jacket with matching leather pants and custom cowboy boots, he had left no doubt as to his Texas roots. After a lavish evening affair, we had walked through the darkened galleries to the East Building offices to retrieve my purse.

Majestic shadows reinterpreted the priceless art as we had moved along the marble halls, deadly quiet except for the clicking of my high heels on stone. Trespassing through this cavernous mausoleum at night filled with the world's masterpieces had been a perfect way to start an affair. Phillip was exciting, successful, charming. But why did he keep me at a distance?

13

Georgetown
Lexington, Virginia

Dressed and ready to go, I drank my morning coffee at the kitchen island. I fixed poached eggs and waffles from the freezer, popped in the toaster, to fortify myself for the day's drive.

My trip to Oklahoma hadn't solved anything but I was glad I went. While my mother's house drove me crazy, it was affirming to spend time with her and Godiva. Maybe one of these days after I was settled into my job, I could bring Godiva back. Maybe I should move my mother and Godiva to Washington. Wait. The mere thought of getting her house ready to put on the market exhausted me. And I wasn't sure she would want give up Lake Aluma. Come to think of it, I'm not sure I wanted to give up Lake Aluma. We moved around so much growing up—nine cities from first grade to twelfth—Lake Aluma had become the only permanent home we could claim. What was I thinking?

It wasn't the first time I had chosen to solve one of my mother's 'problems' as displacement activity to avoid dealing with the huge problems looming large and ominous in my own life.

On top of the lawsuit, the fundraising goals I needed to reach didn't disappear because my world had been turned upside down, literally and figuratively. With all the distractions of the last couple of weeks, I was miserably behind. I needed a few hundred thousand dollars to make Gallery benchmarks for this quarter.

After waving goodbye to the F.B.I. guys now stationed around my townhouse, I closed the front door and walked to my parked car around the corner. I threw my purse into the front seat and pointed my Volvo toward I-66 West.

Usually donors came to the museum. I gave them a tour, possibly took them to lunch in the Refectory, and followed up with a letter. 'The Ask' or request for a contribution was included in my letter or came later in a face-to-face meeting for a more substantial commitment. Occasionally I went to them.

There were two families in southwest Virginia that had the capacity to do something substantial for the Gallery, if so inclined. In this case, I looked forward to the trip. The luscious hills of Lexington, home of Washington & Lee University, was where Bill Trevor and I had met twenty-one years ago.

Bill, in his second year of law school at UVA, was

back visiting his fraternity brothers at "the farmhouse" where W&L Kappa Sigs partied between stints of rigorous studying. I was there as the date of a freshman, a nice guy I knew from Langley High School where I was a senior. Bored with the buttoned down W&L boys and their perfectly dressed pony-tailed fillies, I was drawn to two fellows in the tiny bare foyer engaged in uproarious laughter. The one with the shock of dark hair and crystal blue eyes intrigued me. His toothbrush stuck out of the pocket of his pale blue jean jacket was the sort of eccentricity I liked. When he roared away on his BSA motorcycle, I had no idea that I'd ever see him again. But I knew I'd never forget him.

A month later when we saw each other across the room at another party, the attraction was immediate and mutual. So began our passionate love affair. I was seventeen. Bill was twenty-one. We wrote letters, lots of them. I visited him in Charlottesville. He visited me at my parent's home in McLean, when Daddy was stationed at the Pentagon.

Seared into my memory was how humiliated I was when I took Bill downstairs to show him where he would be staying. I had forgotten that my mother had painted the stairs. Partially painted the stairs. Having been distracted no doubt by some family crisis, she had interrupted her paint project, leaving drips of white paint dried in stark contrast against the dark brown wood of the risers. Those unfinished steps compared to Bill's elegant family home, which I would see shortly, exemplified the vast difference in our upbringings.

In due time Bill's mother wrote my parents to invite me to meet the family. Bill had told me his parents had 'a fat house.' What could have prepared me to see Whittington Plantation for the first time? A world I had never seen and yet was accepted into. One year later Bill would be dead on the side of a road.

Yellow and stiff, Bill's letters with their original envelopes were tied carefully together with a satin ribbon and tucked into the back of my dresser drawer. Every once in a while I pulled them out and reread them.

With all my reminiscing, the drive down went by in a flash. I had reached Lexington's quaint main street. My first call was on a prominent couple who lived downtown in an exquisite home that had been a bank in the nineteenth century. The bars on the windows were still intact, the hardwood floors buffed to a high gloss. Their collection of antiques, including antique silver, was over the top. My favorite silver pieces were by Hester Bateman. Noting my interest, my prospective donor—I called him Mr. Antique—told me Hester's story.

"After Hester Bateman's husband died, she had to raise their five children on her own. She was a smart businesswoman even though she was illiterate. But she registered her hallmark in 1761 at age fifty-two and produced thirty thousand pieces of silver over her career to become the most famous female silversmith in history."

"How fascinating." I couldn't talk about silver all day. I had to make 'the Ask.' "Thank you for having me in your home. I'd like to invite you to become a member of the National Gallery by joining the Circle. We have fabulous events in conjunction with our exhibitions. Here are our giving levels." I handed them the beautiful Gallery brochure showing gift levels from $1,000 to $20,000. "At the leadership level, you would be invited to private lunches and dinner with the director and our curators." With all their fabulous possessions, obviously great wealth, I thought surely Mr. and Mrs. Antique would give to the Gallery. I was learning to read people's subtle body language when I mentioned the possibility of giving a gift to the Gallery. Mr. and Mrs. Antique both stiffened when the subject of money came up, *parting with their money,* that is. And then the excuses cascaded like a waterfall.

"We would love to support the National Gallery but we are so overloaded and committed right now," Mrs. Antique said, trying hard to sound sincere. "Next month we're set to go to Europe for several weeks. And after that we are hosting the Virginia Hunt Club. Perhaps after the season is over, we could ring you."

In development conferences we were told to look for donors with modest homes and rusty Chevrolets. They were the ones with money to give. People with expensive tastes often were so busy getting and spending that they didn't give philanthropically.

My next call was on the owners of a soft drink distributorship covering the tri-state region. My research revealed this family could easily write a seven-figure check.

I drove past what I thought was the address, but all I saw was a small house up the hill nestled among scraggly trees. I circled back around but still could not find the impressive mansion I expected. Maybe this was the manager's house, although it hardly looked good enough for that. At least they would know where the richest family in the county lived. I drove up to the dilapidated home. Old appliances covered the front porch. As I was getting out of my car, a woman came out of the back door.

"Miss Clermont?"

"Mrs. Troy?" I said, straining to disguise my shock.

"Yes, come in," Mrs. Troy said in a sweet voice as she held open the screen door.

We entered her house through the kitchen. I had never seen such a kitchen except in movies, circa 1950. She led me through the dining room—the table had a single gourd in the middle of a crocheted cloth—and into the living room. The plastic blinds, completely closed, shut out the day's brilliant sunshine. In the place of a sofa, mattresses were stacked five feet high against one wall with a sheet over them. In the opposite corner, a single rocking chair sat next to a one TV tray and on it, one can of Pepsi Cola. A dining room chair occupied the other corner. The only other object in the room was a huge television set. Mrs. Troy directed me to sit down. She sat in the rocker. I took the wooden chair on the opposite side of the room. I had stepped into a David Byrne film.

"You are so nice to come all this way to see us. Are you looking for art to display at the museum?"

The irony of that question when there was no art in her home was Twilight Zone alarming. I suppressed a smile. "No, Mrs. Troy. Actually I help raise funds for the National Gallery so that our curators can purchase works of art to add to the nation's collection. You are Mrs. Alfred Troy?"

"Oh, yes. Mrs. Alfred Troy the sixth. We decided not to name any of our boys after Alfred. Getting too close to Henry the eighth." She laughed.

"Well, of course." I could hear the Twilight Zone theme song.

"Oh, here's Alfred in the flesh," Mrs. Troy announced.

Mr. Troy's uneven gait gave an immediate clue to his clubfoot. He wore a white shirt, no tie, black pants, white socks, black shoes. His skin had not been exposed to the sun for many years. The man of the house did not sit but leaned against the mattresses. I explained the purpose of my visit.

"Well, Miss Clermont, I'm not saying 'hell no,' but right now I have to say 'no.' With all the stupid talk about how bad sugar is, sales have been down. Way down."

A little more chit chat ensued about how their sons

and daughters "lived right down the street." I thanked them for their time. They invited me back if "you're ever in the area again." I tried not to scatter gravel when I gunned my car engine. They obviously didn't have many fundraisers hounding them. If Harvard graduates were asked to invent the most successful ruse to get rid of development officers, that scene was it.

A whole day gone and I hadn't raised a penny for the Gallery.

14

National Gallery of Art
Washington, D.C.

A call from a security guard interrupted our morning staff meeting. Theodore Pennington was downstairs. I clipped on my NGA badge and headed to the elevator bank. I was surprised Theo hadn't set up an appointment first.

"Theo," I greeted him. He was only mildly more presentable than when I had met him in Boston. "I didn't know you were going to be in Washington."

"Well, you see, I was here on other business. I've brought this little painting." He patted his black portfolio. "Maybe we should take it straight to your Conservation Department."

"Sure. Let me call them and let them know we're coming."

"Jolly good," Theodore said as he pushed his smudged glasses back on his nose.

As we walked toward the West Building, I called

Conservation.

I held up my badge in front of the unmarked doors letting us into one of the many secret cave-like spaces unseen by the public. The wide hall was bare except for exhibition posters, dollies, and wooden frames.

Caroline Higgins-McNiece greeted us. Her petite figure and oversized red glasses belied her thirty years of restoration experience. Caroline's hair, the color of Bing cherries, was as distinctive as her enunciation.

"Caroline, this is Theodore Pennington. He is interested in giving the Gallery a Matisse painting. Theo, Caroline is head of Conservation."

"Hello, Mr. Pennington. I look forward to examining your painting. Do you have its provenance papers with you?"

"Well, you see, my mother gave this to me right before she died and unfortunately her house burned shortly thereafter." Theo unzipped his portfolio and removed the colorful painting he had shown me in Boston, a woman asleep, her head resting on a table.

Caroline cleared her throat and drew herself up. "Do you know where she purchased the painting?" She peered at the swirls of paint rather than directly at Theodore Pennington.

"I'm afraid I don't. Mummy and I weren't on speaking terms until the end. The only thing she told me about the Matisse was that Hermann Goering had taken it from the Jeu de Paume and traded it with an art dealer for something else. And after that, the painting changed owners a few times before my mother bought it."

Caroline adjusted her red frames and rested her hand on her chin. "Where did your mother live? That might help us trace the ownership," Caroline looked at Theo.

"In London," he answered.

"This will slow down the process considerably as we research all pertinent catalogues."

"No rush," Theo said. "I'll be on my way then. I hope it's something the museum will treasure. It would make mummy, God bless her soul, quite pleased. Cheerio."

"Millicent," Caroline said as I led Theo out, "if you have a minute, I've got something interesting to show you on the painting from Whittington."

A strange look appeared on Theo's face. And a weird feeling came over me that I couldn't explain.

Caroline made sure Theodore was out of Conservation before she spoke. "Millicent, there is a Matisse in the Gallery's collection that was taken by Goering from the Jeu de Paume that bears a striking resemblance to Pennington's painting. I am not aware of any other studies Matisse did of *Sleeping Woman*. Maybe he did paint other versions and both paintings were in the Jeu de Paume. I'll check it out. This guy has a lot of gumption to try to give the National Gallery a painting without any provenance documentation."

"I should have asked for that first," I muttered. "I got carried away with it being a Matisse. Guess I'm a bit naïve."

"You'll lose that soon enough." Caroline walked over to a cabinet, unlocked it, and placed Lee's painting on one of the worktables. It was bizarre seeing Lee's painting here at the Gallery and not in the library at Whittington.

"Once we remove the surface dirt and grime," she explained, "we test the painting's authenticity by determining the age of the paint. If paint hasn't had years to dry, alcohol will dissolve it. If a forger used gelatin glue to make a painting look old, water will soften the glue. The one substance that eludes both the alcohol and water tests is Bakelite."

"Bakelite? You mean the material used to make telephones and toys?"

"Yes. The infamous World War II forger Han van Meegeren would start with a seventeenth century painting. He would scrape off the old image but leave the fine lines, or cracks, what we call age crackle or *craqueleur.* He mixed Bakelite into his pigments, applied the paint to the canvas then baked it in his makeshift oven. Once it hardened, Van Meegeren's forgery had the appearance of an old painting that passed the usual tests that detect forgeries. He was quite meticulous. He also used natural aquamarine blue that Dutch painters used in the seventeenth century. That is, until it was unavailable during the war. Then he used cobalt blue, a pigment not discovered until the nineteenth century and readily detectible. But by that time, he had fooled so many people."

"For all that trouble, you'd think he would have spent his time learning to paint better."

"You'd think," Caroline agreed.

"But couldn't art experts see through Van Meegeren's guise?"

"That's what is so fascinating. It's not that Van Meegeren's paintings were so great but they created the illusion of greatness. He painted what people wanted to see. During World War II with Hitler in power, paintings in the style of Vermeer with Germanic similarities were in great demand. Hermann Goering traded a hundred and fifty paintings for one Vermeer, or what he thought was a Vermeer. It was another forgery by Van Meegeren. Some of the world's most sophisticated art dealers, museum curators, and collectors, including our own Andrew Mellon, bought into Van Meegeren's web of deceit. The Boijmans Museum in Rottingham gave star rating in its 1938 Dutch exhibition to a supposed Vermeer, *The Supper at Emmaus,* only to find out later it was also a Van Meegeren forgery. It goes to show how frenzied the art market was during the war."

"You're not saying Lee Trevor's painting is a fake, are you?" I asked anxiously.

"We don't know yet. The canvas was cut down. The signature, if there was one, is missing. Many paintings during the war were altered purposely or carelessly. But Vermeer did not sign all his paintings, and when he did, he used different variations of his signature. Signatures don't always tell us a lot. Forgers are good at copying a signature."

"Can you tell if it is an authentic Dutch painting from the seventeenth century?"

"We won't know without further testing. But the secret code in the overpainting was probably added in the last fifty to sixty years," Caroline said casually.

"Secret code?" I was stunned.

"Paint with high lead content appears white in an X-ray." Caroline placed an X-ray film up on a lighted panel as in a doctor's office. "Do you see these tiny numbers and letters in the lower left hand corner?"

I peered at the white figures. "What do they mean?"

"We don't know yet. David Perry is on his way from California to help us with this."

My heart leaped and my face turned hot. A reaction that floored me.

15

Washington D.C.

Phillip Gray had asked me to meet him at Ten Penn, a popular Asian restaurant on the corner of Pennsylvania Avenue and 10th Street. I came straight from the Gallery and arrived before six. It wasn't the first time I had rearranged my calendar to accommodate Phillip's last minute invitations. Although over half my wardrobe was black, today I had decided to wear royal purple, my favorite color. My black patent leather high heels would kill me later but were a small price to pay to feel sexy.

I pulled out Phillip's latest book from my purse. At 6:15 p.m. I ordered a second glass of wine and sighed. Maybe Diane was right. Phillip was not the one. But he was the only one calling. At 6:35 p.m. Phillip strolled in, his leather fringe jacket flapping and his cowboy boots clicking.

"Sorry I'm late." He said as he brush kissed me on the cheek. The bartender came over immediately. You could tell she wanted to see if Phillip might be Richard Gere. It happened all the time. He ordered his usual martini.

"Oh, no problem. I was deep into your book. How was the book signing?" I asked.

"Great. Good crowd. Not one of those dreadfully boring ones," Phillip said.

"I can't imagine going through all that. You must love it."

"Authors have to promote and market their own books. Publishers sure as hell don't do it these days. I like the writing part. Good writing is like panning for gold. Shake, shake, shake until the dirt falls out and only shiny nuggets remain."

"You have obviously found your calling," I said in genuine admiration.

"The days of signing hard cover books are on their way out. My next book will probably be an e-book and I'll have an interview streamed on a podcast. Who knows how long bookstores can stay in business?"

"That's a depressing thought. I love books and bookstores."

"Life in the big city." With a big grin, he took the olive out of his glass and ate it.

Over dinner I tried to tell him about the painting, the lawsuit, my predicament.

"Stop worrying," he said, cutting me off. "It'll work out. Want some yacht coffee?" That was our name for coffee with Courvoisier, our take on the Navy's drink of coffee and bourbon they called boat coffee.

"Sure." I was resigned to the fact that Phillip took little interest in what concerned me. "I've got two tickets to the Kennedy Center weekend after next. Want to come?" I asked tentatively.

"Gosh, wish I could. Some friends are throwing a book signing party for me in Dallas. Dreary types or I'd invite you."

"Well, it was just a thought," I mumbled, the designer doormat reappearing. What was wrong with this picture? Why didn't we ever go out on the weekends? When was he going to invite me to Dallas? Why did I think this relationship was going anywhere?

We took a cab back to my townhouse. Fred and Pete, the F.B.I. guys, were posted outside.

"How long do you have to have those geeks around?" Phillip sneered at my protectors.

"Those geeks, as you call them, want to make sure someone doesn't kill me."

"Really, Millicent. Whoever broke into your house didn't find what they were looking for. Seems overkill to me. No pun intended."

"It's not my decision. Anyway, it was scary to find my home turned upside down. I felt violated."

"Don't think about it." He led me upstairs. Our lovemaking used to be fast and exciting. Now it was fast. The man could charm. Like snakes and bracelets.

"I've got an early breakfast with my agent," he said this time. Phillip never stayed the night.

16

Washington D.C.

David Perry looked carefully at the X-rays of Lee's painting clipped to the light panels in the Gallery's windowless Conservation Department.

"I thought your specialty was the art market during World War II," I said, peering at the black vinyl image of the Dutch painting. David's cologne was intoxicating. His purple bow tie, another Cupid arrow.

"It is. But that includes not only the buying and selling, but the making and selling of forgeries, and more rarely, codes that were overpainted on certain pieces," David explained.

"Why would someone put a code on a painting?"

"Two reasons. One, it's an unlikely place and, two, a painting is more easily traced than a piece of paper or other medium if it is lost. Actually a rather clever way to preserve a code. Also, one needs an X-ray machine to discover it."

"Do you have any idea what it means?" I asked,

worried what I was going to tell Lee Trevor about this new development concerning her painting.

"I'm fast but not that fast." David shifted his gaze off the X-rays and looked directly at me. He hesitated for a moment and gave a slight smile. I melted.

It was close to five o'clock. The Gallery would be closing soon. I didn't want to go to my townhouse and be there by myself and I couldn't call Andrew. He was out with his friend from Palm Beach.

"David, would you like to have a quick dinner with me? There's a great French restaurant on Wisconsin."

"Great idea," David said as he switched off the light panels behind the X-rays films. "Let's go."

"Hi, George. Two for dinner," David announced to the maître d' at Bistro Lepic.

"You've obviously been here." I said, amused.

"Several times. It's one of my favorite restaurants in Washington." Candles glowed as we were led to our table.

"Would you care for a glass of red wine?" David asked.

"I would love that."

David ordered a nice bottle of Cabernet and it was delivered in an instant.

"Cheers," David said as he clicked my glass. "Here's to solving another art mystery."

"Cheers," I repeated, feeling more optimistic. I took a sip of the garnet liquid, relaxing into the evening. We were handed the menus. "Do you have any children, David?" Safe first question.

"I have two daughters and two sons. They live on the West coast from San Diego to Seattle." David scanned his menu and ordered.

I ordered the same thing, salmon.

"Their mother died from cancer three years ago." The rim about David's eyes caught a hint of red.

"I'm so sorry."

"But I get to see my children often," David said with a lighter tone. "And my work keeps me busy. What about you, Millicent? Any children?"

"No. No children. I wanted them. My husband didn't, at least not with me. He remarried soon after our divorce." My lips were tight.

"He was a fool to let you get away. But I'm glad he did."

I smiled and lifted my eyebrows, grateful for the compliment and ready to talk about something else. "How did you get interested in the World War II art market?"

"I was reading about the Alt Aussee salt mines where the Nazis stored thousands of pieces of art as the war escalated. The mines turned out to be perfect for properly storing and preserving valuable paintings, exactly the right temperature and humidity. That's what got me hooked. And then studying the forgeries of Han van Meegeren, handing his work off as Vermeers and getting away with it."

I'd never heard of Han van Meegeren until this week and now twice. "Caroline was talking about Van Meegeren earlier this week."

"He was quite a character. He was arrested after the war for selling cultural treasures to the Nazis. To avoid death he had to prove he was a liar and a cheat. He tells the truth for once, that he tricked Goering and sold him a fake. But no one believed him. While in custody, he was ordered to paint a fake Vermeer which he relished. Instead of being sentenced to death, he received only a year prison sentence. He died of a heart attack before serving one day."

"You seem to be pretty passionate about it."

"Art is endlessly fascinating—the creation of it, the preservation of it, and the forgery of it which takes a sophisticated understanding of all three. The world will always have forgers, but I want to say to them- use all your knowledge to create something unique of your own."

David's looked at me—from my eyes to my mouth to my hair, sending sensations all over me. Why doesn't Phillip have this effect on me? Better not have any more to drink or I might do something stupid.

During dinner, David's cell phone rang. I could hear a woman's voice on the other end.

"Excuse me," David said to me. "Hi, Jessica. Yes, love. May I call you back when I get to my hotel? I love you, too."

Obviously someone he's involved with. Good thing I didn't embarrass myself with some ridiculous invitation.

"Well, I better be getting home. I enjoyed our dinner," I said.

"Not more than I did."

"We could get a cab together and I'll hop out at my townhouse on N Street," I offered.

"Perfect. I'm around the corner at the Four Seasons."

"Well, guess I'll see you at the Gallery tomorrow." Seeing David the next day would be something I could look forward to.

"Actually I'm flying back to California in the morning."

His remark made my heart sink.

When we reached my place, an F.B.I. agent was standing on my steps.

"Are you expecting someone?" David asked.

"That's one of my F.B.I. watchdogs."

"You have F.B.I. surveillance?"

"My home was broken into a few days ago. They didn't steal anything but they sure made a mess."

"Millicent, what a terrible thing to happen to you. Are you okay staying alone? Is it related to the painting?"

"I don't know. But I'm fine. These guys will protect me. Thank you for dinner, David. It was lovely."

"The pleasure was all mine." David looked at me in such an earnest, sweet way I wanted to kiss him.

I shook his hand and electricity shot through me. "Good night, David."

17

National Gallery of Art
Washington, D.C.

Laura Young, a researcher in Curatorial Records, met me in the Refectory on the seventh floor at 10 a.m. Staff breaks were a good way to chat with colleagues we didn't see during the course of our busy days. We were either tucked in our offices or showing guests around the 271,000 square feet of exhibition space.

"Hi, Millicent. Want to go out on the terrace?" Laura offered.

"Always," I said. The Refectory Terrace overlooking the National Mall, with the Capitol to the left and the Washington Monument to the right, was my favorite spot. The morning haze made a delicate watercolor of the view.

"Laura, I want to educate myself on World War II art confiscation. What books do you recommend?" No doubt news of the lawsuit had circulated throughout the Gallery staff so I maintained eye contact solely on Laura.

"*Rape of Europa* by Lynn Nicolas is the definitive work. You'll want to read that for sure. There is also a DVD of the same title, which is good. You can rent it from Netflix. Another really good book is *The AAM Guide to Provenance Research* that the American Association of Museums published in 2001. The Museum Store might have it, but you can also order it through Amazon. Oh, another resource for you, someone who is a peripatetic Google and very willing to help, is art historian David Perry from San Diego. "

I nearly dropped my coffee cup. I looked inside the Refectory to regain my composure.

"There's Paul and my donors," I said. "Catch you later. Thanks so much, Laura."

I greeted the donors I had invited for "Lunch with a Curator," a program I had set up to cultivate major contributors to the museum. My curator for the day happened to be Paul Morton. He was talking with the two couples I had brought into the Circle, one of the museum's giving groups. The couple from Maryland had invested with Bernie Madoff so it was unlikely the Gallery would see any more major gifts there. The other couple was from a publishing family. If fundraising became any harder, I might as well retire to write the great American novel.

"Let's go through the buffet," I said to them. "Then over lunch Paul will tell us about one of the greatest Dutch painters of all time."

When we were seated with our plates, Paul began his remarks. "Johannes Vermeer was born in 1632 in Delft, a small town between The Hague and Rotterdam. His father was a silk weaver, an innkeeper, and an art dealer. Vermeer inherited his father's businesses and registered as a master painter in 1653. While he was a respected artist, Vermeer was not recognized as an artistic genius until much later.

"Vermeer was not prolific," he continued as we ate. "He produced only thirty-five known works his entire life. But what jewels he created. He was a master of light and shadow, his work is serene and timeless, his paintings are mysterious and intimate with his use of pearls, letters, and maps. One of his most engaging images, *The Girl with the Pearl Earring*, inspired the book and movie a few years ago."

We all nodded in recognition. I was glad the luncheon was going well.

"Another Vermeer painting," Paul added, "*The Girl with the Red Hat*, which we will see in a few minutes, was one of the first paintings purchased by Andrew Mellon, who of course created the National Gallery. Ironically, at the same time Andrew Mellon was giving his collection to the citizens of the United States, Hitler was stealing art from European citizens."

We finished our lunch and walked over to the West Building. Upon entering the Dutch Galleries we gazed at

The Girl with the Red Hat.

Paul Morton was the quintessential professor with his signature bow tie and horn-rimmed glasses, which he removed and inserted, after a couple of tries, into the pocket of his tweed jacket. He resumed his remarks. "Vermeer was sensitive to the role that color plays in creating accents and mood. In many of his paintings, he used the primary palette of yellow and blue to enhance the feeling of serenity he sought. However, in *The Girl with the Red Hat*, he placed the flame-red hat smartly on the young girl's head evoking vibrancy and life.

"To think of the history of this three hundred and fifty year old painting that is little more than nine inches by seven inches is staggering. After all this time, *The Girl with the Red Hat* still holds her own and could easily be worth a hundred million dollars."

We all let out a polite gasp. *Wow.*

"Next to *The Girl with the Red Hat* is my favorite painting, *Woman Holding a Balance*. On her table are pearl necklaces, behind her a painting within a painting, the *Last Judgment*. The woman, possibly expecting a child, holds the delicate balance in her hand asking us to weigh the material world against the spiritual."

As Paul talked I took notice of my donors. The man from the publishing firm had on an expensive jacket but the collar stood out from his neck, it didn't lie flat. His wife's pantsuit fit her well but was not her color. She should stay away from brown; black or dark blue would be more flattering. And bolder jewelry would help give her some pizazz. The man and wife who had invested with Bernie Madoff were perfect as far as their clothes and accessories. She was carrying a beautiful purse and her clothes—blue and yellow—matched her hair and eyes, alá Diane Sawyer. But they were edgy behind their veneer of 'everything's fine.'

"The last Vermeer painting we'll talk about today is *A Lady Writing*," Paul said as he moved to another framed work in the Dutch Galleries. "In this one, the woman is wearing a yellow satin jacket trimmed in ermine. Vermeer used this jacket many times in his paintings. It might have been his wife's jacket. We don't know for sure. Unfortunately, Vermeer died horribly in debt in 1675 leaving his wife and eleven children penniless. His widow had to sell all they had."

The investors folded their arms over their chests simultaneously.

"It was not until the late nineteenth century," Paul continued, "when a French art critic named Étienne-Joseph Théophile Thoré changed Vermeer's standing in the art world. Thoré, under the pseudonym of William Bürger, wrote rave reviews of Vermeer's genius after searching for his work throughout Europe. And for the first time Vermeer became internationally known and appreciated."

"It is so sad that the last part of Vermeer's life was so hard," I said.

"Like many artists, unfortunately," Paul concluded.

We thanked Paul for his interesting talk and then I escorted my donors through the West Building entrance on Constitution Avenue. "I hope to see you at our Circle reception next month. We're opening a spectacular Florence exhibit."

The investors gave me twisted smiles and nodded. The publishing couple thanked me but didn't commit. I watched the four of them walk away in their designer clothes and expensive jewelry not expecting to see them again. They knew I would be asking them for another five-figure gift.

I headed back to my office. Another day without a commitment or check to the Gallery. Once in the East Building, I stopped into Paul's office on the fifth floor to thank him for his time today.

"Why did Hitler and the Nazis covet Vermeer so much?" I asked Paul. "Vermeer painted such delicate scenes. So many were domestic scenes with women. It's surprising that Vermeer was a favorite of Hitler and Goering."

"After Vermeer became internationally known with William Bürger's help," Paul said taking off his glasses and trying to find their home in his jacket, "his work was highly sought after. Because there were so few known works attributed to Vermeer, his existing paintings were even more valuable. The other factor in play was the Nazis' promotion of art that represented the Aryan culture, meaning anything with a Germanic heritage. Vermeer fit the bill. Hitler and Goering competed with each other, although Goering was smart enough to never cross Hitler. It was a ripe situation for Han van Meegeren to create Vermeer forgeries."

"How can you tell if a painting is a fake or not?" I asked.

"It's a combination of scientific analysis and intuition. The scientific part is pretty straightforward. But after all the scientific, chemical, quantitative research and analysis, experts still have to have an intuitive sense about the painting in question... a *qualitative* sense that the particular piece was produced by the artist."

"But Han van Meegeren fooled everyone?"

"He was good, although if you compare his 'Vermeers' to the real Vermeers, it is clear who the master painter is. But during World War II, the art world was in chaos and there were those who wanted to believe Van Meegeren's forgeries were real."

"You used the word forgery. Is that the same as a fake?" I asked.

"Not technically, but the terms 'fake' and 'forgery' are still used interchangeably," Paul said. "A forgery is presented as real, an authentic work by the purported artist. A fake is a copy. There was a recent case that illustrates the difference. For publicity purposes, an illustrator had copied an original Remington and signed it with his own signature, not trying to deceive the public.

That painting was a fake not a forgery. Then another artist took the fake Remington, overpainted the illustrator's signature with a forged Remington signature, and passed it off as the real thing. That made it a forgery. The forged signature was discovered from a tiny paint sample the size of a grain of sand."

"Interesting. Thanks, Paul. See you later." I waved myself out of his office.

I prayed that Lee's painting was a real Vermeer and not a forgery by Han van Meegeren. But I had no control over that issue. However, maybe I could do something about the lawsuit.

18

Paris

I knew it was a huge risk. But if I didn't try it, if I didn't bend the rules, I might lose Lee. My job was already on the line, so what difference would it make if I raised the stakes? If my plan failed and I spent all my savings for nothing, then at least I could say I tried everything to help Lee. I prayed for courage to ask David if he would go to Paris with me to talk to the plaintiffs who were suing us. Without any of their lawyers or ours at the meeting. I wanted to appeal to them directly to see if they would agree to a continuance.

To my surprise, David said yes sooner than I had expected. I offered to pay for his airfare but he refused. Not only that, he said he had complimentary rooms at a Paris hotel so I wouldn't be out for lodging. I took this as a divine sign that my plan might work.

I asked John Peale if I could have two days off, a Friday and the next Monday. He thought I needed a vacation given the events of the last few weeks.

I couldn't believe I was en route to Paris sitting next to David Perry. Rugged gorgeous. My heart expanded as I looked out the plane's window—cotton-ball clouds on blue with a hint of pink à la Georgia O'Keefe.

"Would you care for champagne?" the attractive French flight attendant said.

"It's my favorite. Merci beaucoup," I said, hoping my French did not grate on her ears.

David took a glass too, his eyes luminous aquamarine in the high altitude light.

"Have you been to Paris?" I asked him.

"Many times. I studied at the Sorbonne."

Obviously my stereotype of boring college professor was wrong.

"Thank you so much for coming with me," I said as I looked into his crystalline eyes trying to maintain my composure. "It's a huge risk meeting the plaintiffs. Lawyers hate opposing parties talking to each other. But once the Alexanders hear our side of it, I hope they will back off. At least that's what I'm banking on. Plus I'm curious to find out if they know about the secret code. I figure I can ask for forgiveness later."

"There's only one way to find out," David clicked our champagne glasses putting me immediately at ease.

"What do you think the code might mean?" I asked.

"It could mean anything. Historically, secret codes

revealed strategies in war, formulas for an invention, or hiding places of treasures. Since we think the Nazis stole the painting, my assumption is that an art restorer was directed to apply the code."

"Do you think Baader knows what it means?"

"My bet is that he knows it's there but needed to have it X-rayed to find out what it means," David said.

"Why didn't he get it X-rayed when he had it?"

"You'd think he would have. Immediately. But trying to figure out the criminal mind is a frustrating exercise in futility. Criminals can be so brilliant on the one hand and incredibly stupid on the other."

"What about Pet Wilde? What do you think he knows?"

"He is clever. From what Haywood has said about him, he knows how to slip out of sticky situations. He has been sued over his shady dealings, but no one to date has been able to hold him accountable. Of course, he denied knowing anything about Lee's painting. There was nothing they could charge him with."

After our airplane dinner, David took out his iPad, I pulled out my Daniel Silva paperback, *The Rembrandt Affair.*

"Do you know where the forerunner of the paperback was first published?" David asked.

"No idea. But I bet you do." I admired his handsome face.

"In Venice, the printing capital of the world, at least in the fifteenth century. A Venetian by the name of Aldus Manutius invented the pocket edition so readers could carry books in their sachets. Have you ever been to Venice?"

"Can't say I have."

"I'll have to take you sometime."

Not to appear too eager, I ignored his statement. "Speaking of printing," I began, "I thought it was fascinating that Gutenberg was a goldsmith and invented the printing press based on his knowledge of precious metals."

"Yes," David added, "he made metal forms for each letter of the alphabet not unlike hallmarks in gold and silver."

"I'm beginning to think you know everything," I said.

"Far from it. But I am curious."

"Well, I love printing and I love paper. I'll probably never switch to a Kindle or iPad."

"But I can carry fifty books around with me at a time and no trees died," David countered.

"You can't read that many books on an airplane and those trees were grown to make paper."

"You sound unwavering on that subject."

"That's exactly right," I stared at him with playful anger. "I will defend and promote forever the making of paper and the printing thereon, preferably in Garamond typeface." The champagne was helping me make my point.

"Garamond?" David leaned in.

"The same typeface in Dr. Seuss and Harry Potter books. But's that's not why I like it. I just do. The fact that a Frenchman developed Garamond in the sixteenth century makes it even more wonderful."

"I'm learning all sorts of things from you, Millicent. Now if you'll excuse me, I'm going to catch up on *The New York Times* on my iPad." David turned on his device.

"Yes, I am going back to my paperback," I said with conviction. I found my place in *The Rembrandt Affair* but instead of following Daniel Silva's novel, my mind wandered to what I had read about paper.

Linen paper in the fifteen and sixteenth century was made from linen garments. Everyone wore linen from the aristocracy to the peasants. When their garments wore out, 'rag men' picked them up and took them to the paper factory where they were boiled for two days. The resulting pulp was spread into sheets and pressed between pieces of wool with a device like a wine press to squeeze the water out. Once the sheets dried, the linen paper was ready to sell.

Gutenberg invented the printing press at the same time paper was plentiful and scribes were in short supply following the Black Death. I returned to my novel. I was afraid to go to sleep. Heaven forbid I would wake up with bed head.

Less than seven hours later, a sleepy trip from DeGaulle Airport brought us to Le Grand Hotel across the street from the historic Paris Opera House. Luckily, the hotel checked us in early. Same floor but not next to each other.

"Let me freshen up a bit and I'll meet you downstairs in the hotel restaurant in about an hour." I took a quick shower and changed into my new black pants, short jacket, and high heels. I tied my Hermes scarf, a gift from Gabby, around my neck and headed down stairs.

The name of the hotel restaurant was Café de la Paix, the same as in my painting at home. What a delightful coincidence. I took it as another good sign that this trip was the right course of action. The café opened to the sidewalk. I chose a table outside that David could easily spot.

"Bonjour, Madame." The waiter handed me a menu.

David appeared at the door of the restaurant in a navy jacket, khaki pants, and a crisp white shirt. A little frog leaped in my heart. I waved.

He sat down beside me. "What a beautiful spot. Great people watching."

"I could stay here all day admiring the styles," I said.

David ordered our lunch like a native Frenchman.

"This is exciting, Millicent. To be able to meet the owner of a painting lost to the family for seventy years. And a painting with so many secrets."

"I hope the Alexanders are receptive. To be in the middle of a lawsuit is not my idea of fun. I'm so glad you're here, David."

"So am I." Being with David made me feel everything was going to work out.

The Alexander apartment on Boulevard Saint-Germain was one of Paris' most prestigious addresses. We walked through the ornate Rococo entry and took the *ascenseur* to the sixth floor. I rang the quaint buzzer.

A striking woman with black hair wearing coral silk opened the door.

"Ms. Clermont? Mr. Perry?" she said in her beautiful French accent. "I'm Colette. Please come in."

David and I walked into the exquisite apartment resplendent with antiques and art.

"Please sit down." Colette said. Her dark eyes set in white porcelain skin were movie star quality. A fitted skirt and high heels complemented her shapely legs and defied her age.

I sat in a gorgeous blue silk chair with fancy trim. "Ms. Alexander, thank you for allowing us to visit you. No doubt your lawyers would hate our meeting without them. But to save all of us a lot of time and resources, I wanted you to know our side of the story."

"I'm listening." Colette said as she clasped her hands together.

"As you know, the National Gallery of Art has your

family's painting. It is safe now. Our Conservation Department is carefully examining it. In the sixties, the husband of Mrs. Lee Trevor of Whittington Plantation in Virginia bought the painting not knowing its real provenance, not knowing that Nazis stole your family's painting in 1940." These facts hadn't been verified but I felt the best way to establish rapport was to take their side.

"Our favorite painting and many other family treasures were taken from this very room." Colette lifted her hands. I noticed her nails were short and *sans* polish, the hands of a writer or a pianist. Images of Nazi soldiers tramping through this elegant home popped into my head. My dream popped into my head as well.

"What happened was a travesty," I added "I can't imagine all that your family has gone through. But Mrs. Trevor is a victim too in this situation. I am here to ask you for a continuance so that we can resolve this without going to court."

Colette looked from me to David and then back to me. "As to the painting, I have read of other cases where arrangements have been made. I hope we can come to a mutual agreement. But my brother is an equal heir. Unfortunately, Jacques is not so—how to say—philosophical."

"We would hope to meet with him too," I proposed.

"That will be absolutely necessary, Ms. Clermont," Colette affirmed.

"If you could give us his number, perhaps we could see him later today," David offered.

"Unfortunately not. Jacques is in Jerusalem for a few months," Colette said.

I looked at David with wide eyes. Did this mean we'd have to go to the Holy Land? Oh, well. What's another thousand dollars at this point? I grew up without money; it was a familiar state.

"I will call my brother and find out his schedule. I can call you at your hotel. While you are here, please allow me to show you some of my family's art that was returned after the war. The Nazis stripped our grandparents' entire apartment and took their cherished possessions to the Jeu de Paume. From there some pieces were taken to the Alt Aussee salt mine, which turned out to be a good storage place. Of course, many valuable objets d'art were never recovered, including *Lady in Waiting*."

"Is that the name of the Dutch painting now at the National Gallery?" I had never heard that name.

"Oui. Yes. That is the name of our family's favorite painting by Johannes Vermeer," Collette pronounced.

I nearly fell out of my chair. This delicate painting I had known, or thought I knew, was more than a nice Dutch painting.

"Ms. Alexander," David said, "there is one more matter we would need to discuss with you."

"Oui."

"Your family's painting has a secret code in the overpainting. Do you know anything about this?" David asked.

Colette stiffened. "No, I've not heard of any secret message."

"We think it was applied seventy years ago, about the time the painting was taken. This is not unheard of. As you know, many paintings were altered in one way or another during the war."

"What does it mean?" Colette looked directly at David.

"We haven't broken the code yet. But I wanted to let you know of its existence. It will delay a resolution of the painting."

"We have been waiting so many years," Colette said in a defeated voice. "A few more months won't matter." Colette lowered her head then straightened up. "I am going to Père-Lachaise Cemetery this afternoon to visit my grandparents' tombstone. If you've never been to Père-Lachaise, perhaps you'd care to accompany me. It's the most famous burial place in the world."

"Colette," David said, "if I may call you by your first name, we would be honored to go with you."

19

Père-Lachaise Cemetery
Paris

Colette led the way through the magnificent marble tombstones and mausoleums.

"The cemetery was named after King Louis XIV's confessor, Father Lachaise," Colette said. "The city of Paris acquired it in 1804. It was far from the city at that time, and the city launched a marketing campaign to encourage people to use it. They moved the remains of famous individuals buried elsewhere. Molière's body was transferred in 1817."

We walked in front of a beautiful tombstone covered in a profusion of flowers.

"This one says 'A. Fred. Chopin,'" I said.

"Yes," Colette nodded. "His full name was Frederic François Chopin, so why his stone was etched that way, who knows? When he died at age thirty-nine, his heart was removed according to his wishes, and taken to his hometown of Warsaw. Let's go to Oscar Wilde's gravesite."

"I've always loved Oscar Wilde's writing. The king of

paradoxes," I announced.

Oscar Wilde's tombstone was contemporary with an art deco figure, possibly a stylized angel, in a horizontal position. Covered in flowers, admirers had kissed the marble leaving a hundred red butterflies.

We then came upon an elaborate sarcophagus with male and female figures.

"You know the story of the star-crossed lovers, Abelard and Heloise?" Colette inquired.

David nodded. I shook my head.

"Abelard was hired by Heloise's uncle as her tutor," Colette explained. "They fell in love, had a child, but the uncle was against the union. He had Abelard castrated and sent Heloise to a convent. Abelard and Heloise continued their relationship by letter until Abelard's death in 1142. He was buried at Heloise's convent. She died a short time later, and now they are both buried here, together forever."

David gave me a look that made me want to be buried with him forever.

"The French writer Sidonie Gabrielle Colette is right over there," Colette continued. "She was the first woman given a state funeral in France in 1954. She was known simply as Colette, as you can see on her stone. She was quite controversial. After all, she challenged the subservient role of women in society. I wondered if my parents named me after her, but I never asked them."

Looking around the historic cemetery, I thought of

the many funerals and families represented by the hundreds of tombstones, mausoleums, and sarcophagi. Some had small lambs in stone with the epitaph: "Budded on Earth to Bloom in Heaven."

Then I imagined the entire history of this graveyard captured on film in lapsed speed. Families arriving in black carriages on a white foggy morning, adults and children dressed in black mourning, hats and long dresses, crying or maybe relieved. And then as styles changed from early Victorian hoop skirts and biblets to late Victorian bustles and high necks, from the roaring twenties' straight dresses, bosoms bound but ankles showing, to the 1950s with full skirts and cinched waists. Baggy pants, slim pants, wide ties, narrow ties, hats, no hats, gloves, no gloves, pointed toes, rounded toes, flats, stilettos— the evolution of fashion, the language of clothes.

I wondered if the deceased talked to each other as we did above ground.

Perhaps Molière, one of the earliest 'residents' welcomed Oscar Wilde and Frederic Chopin.

"Oscar, I'm so happy you're here. Finally a person of wit," Molière said.

"One should always stay lively, even after death," Oscar said.

"And, Frederic, how delightful to have you here. I love your Funeral March."

"Ah, yes, Sonata No.2 in B Flat Minor," Frederic said.

At least we're not forgotten in some unmarked grave. And I appreciate the flowers, even if half of them are plastic."

"I abhor the fake ones," Oscar said. "Beauty is not meant to last. And I do wish that angry woman had not broken off the stone penis of my angel, which I understand still serves as a paperweight for the cemetery grounds keeper. God, I would have hated to have been her husband, if she ever had one."

"What I hate are people sitting on my tombstone as if I didn't even exist. The other day a young woman sat down and she wasn't wearing a stitch of undergarments," Chopin said.

"You're complaining, ole chap?" Oscar quipped.

"It's not proper," Chopin replied.

"Oh, you bloody boring man! Loosen up." Colette said.

"Thank God. Another writer of enlightened vision," Oscar said.

"Millicent?" I felt David gently shake me.

"Oh, I was daydreaming." I shook my head.

Colette gestured to a large marble slab with skeletal figures on top. "Here is the monument for those who died at Auschwitz." The bronze figures of starving people were a devastating reminder of the suffering at the hands of the Nazis.

We followed Colette around the corner and gazed upon a beautifully carved angel. On the stone under the angel were the names: Poppie and Gigi Alexander. "We decided to use our nicknames for them," Collette said softly. "Our parents thought our name for Poppie was amusing because it is so close to the French word, Poupèe, which means doll. Poppie's sister founded a doll company in New York in 1923. Have you heard of the Madame Alexander doll?"

"Heard of it? Every little girl in America wanted a Madame Alexander doll," I exclaimed.

"Poppie's sister, Beatrice, was quite the entrepreneur. She led her company until she was ninety years old. And then lived another five years until she was ninety-five. Her grandson worked in the company before they sold it. That's my cousin Bill. He and his wife now live in Greenwich, Connecticut. Jacques and I are fortunate to have family to visit."

"Colette, I know your cousin and his wife," I said astonished.

"You do? Bill and Kathe?" Collette leaned toward me.

"Yes!" I beamed. "They live on Lake Avenue. Kathe is a fabulous artist. What a coincidence." It was then I knew I was right in following my intuition and coming to Paris.

Exuberant, I said goodbye to Colette and told her we would await her call about her brother. I couldn't wait to call my friends in Greenwich. Maybe this would be the tipping point to get Colette and Jacques to agree to a continuance.

My impulse to go to Paris to talk to the Alexanders

had been so strong while at the same time not rational. It was still possible John Peale would fire me for talking to them directly. But now...I wondered if divine intervention had stepped in to line up these seemingly random events.

20

Paris

Once inside my hotel room, I slipped off my clothes and snuggled in the luxurious bed linens. After a short nap, I showered again then smoothed on my Perfect Gardenia body lotion and perfume from Malibu. My slinky black dress, stilettos, pink baroque pearls, and cashmere stole finished my look. I felt French and sexy. All of a sudden, I wasn't as worried about Lee or the lawsuit or anything else. And certainly not Phillip.

David was waiting for me in the lobby bar, a spacious room filled with gorgeous flowers. He had on an ascot with a dark blue jacket. He stood when he saw me.

"My, aren't we French?" I gestured at his neck attire.

"I would never wear this in California, but when in Paris…."

"I couldn't agree more." I smiled and took his arm as we walked out.

The evening was perfect. Flowers overflowing from window boxes on building after building. Boats on the

Seine with their delicate lighting. Paris at night was a natural aphrodisiac.

"Since we're stuck here until we hear about Jacques, would you care to go to dinner at Café Colbert?"

"The restaurant that was in *Something's Gotta Give*?"

"Yes. And the food is actually quite good."

At dinner, David ordered a bottle of Châteauneuf-du-Pape (how did he know it was my favorite?) and we both ordered the grilled salmon.

"It seems Colette is going to be quite easy to deal with," I said.

"Seems that way. Let's hope Jacques is. Otherwise, we've got a problem."

I noticed that David said, "we've got a problem" not "you've got a problem." How long had it been that I had faced problems by myself? Excited about today's meeting, I posed, "So, are we going to Jerusalem?"

"Have you ever been?" David asked.

"No. I haven't."

"It's a remarkable city. Quite a paradox. The center of three world religions and yet one of the least peaceful places on earth."

On the way back to the hotel, we drove past the Eiffel Tower, spectacularly illuminated from top to bottom. No wonder this city with a past turned on a light in every heart. And then we stopped at the Paris Ritz on the Place

Vendome.

"Could I entice you with a drink at Bar Hemingway?" David asked.

"Oui, monsieur." I grinned from pearl earring to earring.

As we walked through the main entrance, I thought of Coco Chanel and Pamela Harriman, both past residents of the Ritz. Mrs. Harriman, once married to Winston Churchill's son, died while she was swimming in its pool. We walked past the restaurant, turned right and proceeded down a long corridor until we arrived at the famous bar named after Ernest Hemingway. I was suprised at how small it was. Only about six tables and the bar. It wouldn't hold more than twenty people.

When the waiter brought our drinks, each drink was adorned with a large flower. My glass of red wine had a gorgeous red rose. David's scotch had a stargazer lily. We toasted to Hemingway's vintage typewriter behind the bar.

"It is wonderful being here with you, Millicent." David's eyes were laser beams into my soul. "I can't imagine a more ideal evening."

Neither could I.

In the taxi going back to our hotel, David took my hand. We rode the rest of the way in silence. Utterly serene, exquisitely exciting silence. We arrived at the hotel, got out of the cab and walked into the lobby. I turned and offered my hand.

"Are you sure you want to call it a night? Don't you want one tiny glass of Veuve Clicquot?" David said.

"You said the magic words. Its 'yellow label' which is actually orange is the only orange I like."

I sat down at a sofa in the lobby bar. David sat down next to me and motioned to a waiter.

"What do you believe are the three most important things a man and a woman should know about each other?" David asked.

"Before they… work together? Before they marry?" Here I was in Paris and this man was asking me for love advice before he marries his precious Jessica, whoever she is.

"Before they get together as a couple."

The waiter delivered two flutes and poured the dew of the goddesses.

"Well," I said, using my business voice, "values. You should know the other person's values … and beliefs. What kind of lifestyle you want … Do you trust each other? Do you love each other? That's probably more than three but I'd start there."

"You sound pretty wise."

"Ask Millie, adviser to the stars." I took a sip of my champagne.

"Do you believe in reincarnation?" David peered at me intently.

I looked at him. I smelled his intoxicating cologne. "Do you?"

His gaze dropped to my mouth and then to my neck and back up to my eyes. Sensations pulsed all through my body. "Yes, I believe we have lived other lives and will live other lives," he said. "I believe when we have a strong attraction to someone it is a past-life remembrance at our deepest level."

"Is that how you felt about Jessica when you met her? The one who called you when we were at Bistro Lepic." I felt my foot jiggle.

"Jessica? My daughter? Well, I guess you could say that." David chuckled.

"Oh. I thought Jessica was the woman you were dating."

"I haven't met anyone since my wife's death. That is, I hadn't met anyone until…"

David took my hand and stood up leaving our half finished glasses. "Let's go where we can talk quietly."

As we left the lobby bar, a hotel staff person handed me an envelope. Inside was a message from Colette Alexander. "Jacques can see you in Jerusalem day after tomorrow. Please call me later for details. Amitiés, Colette."

We looked at each other but didn't say a word as we got into the elevator. Then he pulled me into him and kissed me, a gentle kiss. I could feel every part of him. We fit perfectly, locked pieces in a puzzle. The elevator door opened. We looked to see if anyone was standing there and laughed as we stepped into the empty hall.

David held my hand as we walked toward his room. He slid the room card into the slot and opened the door to his suite. Lights of the city glimmered through the windows. First his tie, my pearls, his shirt, my dress, his hands all over me, his mouth all over me, my hands on his smooth back. Then I was on the bed and he entered me slowly, his eyes into my eyes, and the silky friction of love increasing the pace with such pleasure that I climaxed as he reached that out-of-body state and we lay there man and woman made by God.

Then it happened. I fell in love with David Perry. My *coup de foudre*—the moment I was struck by lightning, according to the French.

How different from my ex-husband's lovemaking, including his remark that "something is wrong with you, you don't have an orgasm during intercourse." And Phillip's lovemaking? A three on a ten-point scale. Obviously, it was the man who made the difference. Why were women so quick to take the blame? I hugged the wonderful man I lay next to and drifted off to a dreamy sleep.

I wished I could have stayed in Paris for a month. But we were leaving the next morning for Jerusalem.

21

Jerusalem

We arrived in Jerusalem in the evening and went straight to the King David Citadel Hotel. We were so exhausted we ordered room service and turned in early. Exhausted but exhilarated.

The next morning David and I had breakfast at the terrace restaurant. We could see the gates of the Old City from our table. After we finished eating, David left to meet with a fellow art historian at Hebrew University. I walked over to the ancient city gates to get a glimpse of a place that had not changed in two thousand years.

The cavernous walkways emitted a dank, stuffy smell. Dozens of toothy dark-skinned salesmen, some in unlit corners, others lucky to have a booth that opened to the skies, offered "special price for you, special price for you today." One of the inside markets shocked me. Skinned animal heads on sticks lined up in a row almost made me sick. I put my scarf up to my nose to buffer the odor and walked through as quickly as I could. I finally made it to an outside portal and took a deep breath of fresh air.

Ahead of me, the Jacaranda trees had let go of their fragrant flowers, covering the winding streets with their lavender blossoms. I was reveling in this unusual scene when a pretty, female Israeli soldier in a tight uniform with form-fitting pants sauntered down the road carrying an Uzi, her black boots bruising the delicate petals. City of paradoxes, indeed.

I returned to the hotel to change into my suit. "I was transported back two thousand years," I told David.

"Very past-life, this place," he responded.

"I don't think I saw any old souls I used to know."

"Ready to meet Colette's brother?" David took my hand.

I believe I would have followed him anywhere. "I'm ready. And thank you again for picking up the costs of coming here."

"It is my pleasure. Anyway, I needed to see Dr. Freedman. It saved us both an extra trip."

"Lucky me."

En route to Jacques Alexander's office, we saw Roman ruins including the enormous stones the Romans used to build their monuments. To think that men, with the help of only pulleys and animals, moved these gigantic rocks was astonishing. Then in this city of contrasts, we admired the tiny tiles, thousands of half-inch squares of brilliant color forming decorative mosaics on building after building.

Jacques' office was as contemporary as anything in New York. He had the same dramatic coloring as his sister. Dark hair, flecked with gray, dark eyes, smooth skin on an etched facial structure. Handsome as Colette was pretty despite his age. Lithographs with bright splashes of color livened up the black, chrome, and glass furniture: David Hockney and Karl Appel. He had excellent taste.

"Welcome to Jerusalem. How can I help you?" Jacques said in an endearing French accent.

"Mr. Alexander," I said, "I'm sure your sister told you about our meeting with her in Paris regarding your grandparents' painting."

"Yes. We are delighted that this beloved work has surfaced. One spends years hoping and then giving up. Colette and I spent many happy times as children visiting our Poppie and Gigi on Boulevard St.-Germain. Our grandparents loved *Lady in Waiting.* It will be a reunion with an old lost friend."

"Please believe that my mentor, Mrs. Lee Trevor of Whittington Plantation, did not know its true provenance. In fact, I'm quite sure she never knew the name of the painting."

"The problem is, Ms. Clermont, the painting has not been properly attributed to Johannes Vermeer by your authorities. My grandparents understood it to be an authentic Vermeer. That is what they paid for. Now the National Gallery is calling its provenance into question. Therefore, you can understand how frustrating it is for our family to be held in limbo. Obviously, what your experts decide will be the difference between a nice Dutch painting and one of the world's most valuable works of art."

"I can assure you," I said, "the curators at the National Gallery are working as fast and as carefully as they can. Mrs. Trevor in Virginia is also on pins and needles."

"If I may interject here, Mr. Alexander," David said. "There is another perplexing problem that we're working to solve. The secret code in the overpainting."

"Yes, Colette mentioned the secret code." Jacques's eyebrows knitted into a frown.

"A secret code was overpainted in the lower left corner," David said. "The National Gallery asked me to help decipher it. But we are not the only ones who want to know what it means. There are some bad actors who are willing to kill for it."

His words sent a shiver up my spine.

"Please do not tell me this. How long it will take you to break the secret code?" Jacques asked pointedly.

"I have a meeting with an old colleague, Dr. Patrick O'Reilly, at the National Security Agency as soon we land in the States. He is a good friend and an expert in cryptography and steganography."

"I know what cryptography is, but what is

steganography?" I asked.

"Steganography is the science of concealed messages," David said. "It comes from the Greek, meaning 'hidden message.' In ancient Greece, the heads of slaves were tattooed with messages—usually troop movements—and then the secret message was hidden when their hair grew back. Invisible ink falls in this category. Cryptography is when the message itself is scrambled and unintelligible without its code. The Dutch painting has both. An encrypted message also hidden in the overpainting."

"Please keep me abreast of your findings," Jacques said. "Time is of the essence. I believe that's a term of law you understand. To expedite your research, allow me to give you a copy of the provenance papers on *Lady in Waiting*. And, Millicent, please give Bill and Kathe our best regards."

We left with a sense of excitement and urgency to look at the documents Jacques had given us, and a ray of hope that the personal connection would buy some time.

22

National Security Agency
Fort Meade, Maryland

Our flight from Jerusalem to Dulles Airport wore me out completely. But David made me feel secure and that my future was bright. Including a favorable resolution of Lee's situation. If everything in the Alexanders' provenance papers was accurate, then it settled the ownership of Lee's painting. *Lady in Waiting* belonged to Colette and Jacques. But was it a real Vermeer? And what did the code mean and how soon could we figure that out?

"I'm going straight to the National Security Agency once we land. May I meet you back at your place afterward?" David asked me.

"No way. I want to be there when it's cracked. Is it okay if I come with you?"

"Sure. If you don't make it through security, you can wait for me in the taxi." He kissed me on my nose.

The cab took us to the National Security Agency in

Fort Meade, Maryland, headquarters of the most sophisticated spy organization on the planet. I looked at the sea of cars in the parking lot.

"A whole city works here." I remarked.

"Only about 20,000," David said.

We were scanned, including our irises, and photographed using facial recognition software. The security staff probably knew every known fact of my life. Then a scientist type with a shock of red hair, white shirt buttoned to the top, no tie, walked up flashing a big toothy grin. His badge said "Director, Crypto-electronics."

"Good to see you, David," the big teddy bear said as he hugged David.

"Patrick, it's good to see you. You haven't aged a bit."

"It's the ale I drink, laddy. That and my seven children keep me young."

"Patrick, this is Millicent Clermont from the National Gallery."

"A bonny lassie, at that," he winked at David. "Are you ready? Let's go back to my spacious digs and get to work."

Patrick led us though the sterile hallways to his office the size of a closet. Remembering the Yale Law School offices I once visited, his could have been a candidate. Books, files, and papers on every surface in total chaos. He took a stack of papers off two chairs and motioned us to sit. "Show me what you got."

David handed Patrick a copy of the X-ray. "As you

can see, the secret code overpainted on Mrs. Trevor's painting shows the letters NSIM and then the numbers 880099."

"A short code. Shouldn't be too hard to figure out." Patrick entered the code into his computer.

"That's a funny looking machine," I said pointing to a machine on his credenza I thought maybe was an old-fashioned typewriter.

"This little antique, m'dear, is a vintage Enigma machine used by the Nazis to send and decipher secret messages during World War II," Patrick explained. "Today we use computer software to break codes. Secret codes created today would be in the form of microdots and digital watermarks. David, what have you been up to lately? You look a hell of a lot better than when I saw you last."

"Oh, a little of this, a little of that. Things have been looking up lately." David looked at me. Warmth flooded my entire being.

Patrick frowned at his computer screen and then at David. "Nothing's coming up. Give me a little more time to work on this. Can I call you on a secure line?"

"Sure." David scribbled a number on a small piece of paper. "Call me on this number."

The guards gave us back our passports, driver's licenses, and luggage and escorted us out the door.

"It's a pretty impressive place," I said as we headed back to Washington.

"The N.S.A. has the capacity to intercept and download electronic communications equal to the contents of the Library of Congress. Every six hours."

In forty-five minutes we arrived in Georgetown. It was good to be home. David carried in my bag and his and dropped them in the foyer. Something about that seemed right.

I checked my phone messages and noticed several from Phillip. One from my mother. Several from the Gallery. I'd listen to those later. My stack of mail that Andrew had collected while I was gone contained the usual mass of junk mail, bills, and— was this for real?—a card from Phillip. Feast or famine. It never failed.

Exhausted as we were, since David had never been to my home I gave him a quick tour.

"What an elegant home, Millicent. What's with this?" he peered at my six columned dollhouse.

"This is one of my passions. A scale model of the oldest structure on the campus of Mary Baldwin College." I turned the dollhouse around on its lazy Susan. "The living room is fashioned after the front hall at Whittington Plantation."

"Quite detailed and intricate. Do the lights work?" David was being polite.

"Of course." I turned the switch and seven tiny chandeliers illuminated their respective rooms. "Oh, a painting has fallen off the wall." I pressed the tiny frame back.

"That's quite a hobby." David's tone of voice confirmed his lack of interest.

His response didn't surprise me. Most men's and some women's expressions glazed over when I mentioned my one-inch-to-one-foot scale model.

We walked upstairs and fell into my four-poster bed, our jet lag hitting us like an avalanche. Now that I was back in my real world, I wondered about Phillip. Before I analyzed that further, I was out.

David was up early the next morning. By the time I walked downstairs, the coffee was brewed, newspapers spread out on the kitchen island.

"It has been great spending these few days with you, Millicent."

"Yes, it's been magical. Now back to reality."

"We create our own reality."

"Pray tell, Professor Perry." I sipped my hot coffee with lots of cream.

"Have you been to California lately?"

"Not lately. Our critical mass of donors is on the East coast."

"We'll have to rustle you up some in the West. My friends on the West Coast would donate to the museum if you asked them."

"Ah, music to my ears."

"In fact, I'll put a little cocktail party together and

you could give an inspiring talk to woo my friends. I'm sure they will be as impressed with you as I am."

Phillip had never offered this.

"You're a charmer."

"Once we solve the mystery of the Whittington painting, we'll plan a party."

"You're on, prince charming."

David showered, dressed, and kissed me goodbye. My heart ached as I watched him get into the taxi. Closing the door, I went upstairs to get ready for work.

As I picked up my purse to leave, Haywood called.

"We got a tip that you may have a bug in your mantle," Haywood said. "Are you going to be there for a few minutes?"

As if I was going to leave. "Of course."

The men in black went right to work scanning my beautifully carved nineteenth century frontispiece.

"Nothing here," one of them said.

"It came from a good source. Something's amiss here," Haywood said. "Sorry, to make you come over here, guys."

Haywood turned to me. "I interviewed Otto Baader today. I thought you'd be interested in what he said."

"You *interviewed* a prisoner, Haywood? Is that what the F.B.I. calls interrogation?"

Haywood ignored my questions.

"Otto Baader is willing to talk if we show him the

X-rays of the Dutch painting. He said there are other people involved."

"Pet Wilde for one!"

"Brilliant, Millicent."

"Don't make fun of me. If you give him the secret code, will he tell you what it means?"

"I don't think he knows."

"I wonder if he misses wearing his wife's clothing."

"I'll ask him next time I see him." With that, Haywood left.

I picked up my ringing telephone.

"Millicent? Someone got access to the Conservation Department last night and poisoned one of the night guards," Caroline said.

"What?" I said in disbelief.

"Whoever it was knew where the security cameras were and how to dismantle them. I think they were after the Vermeer."

"Why do you say that?"

"Because the cabinet I used to store it in had been tampered with."

"They didn't get the painting, did they?" I asked, my breathing heavy.

"No, it was in X-ray. We planned to take more shots so we left it locked up there."

"How's the guard?" I asked.

"He'll be okay. It wasn't a lethal dose, only enough to

give him flu-like symptoms for a few weeks," Caroline explained in her professional demeanor.

"I guess the Gallery is in complete lockdown," I surmised.

"Only Conservation. We don't want the public to know someone can break into the National Gallery of Art. It's bad enough that the Secret Service knows. The First Lady is on her way over. No way was the director going to tell Michelle she couldn't come today."

23

National Gallery of Art
Washington D.C.

I took the Metro, exiting at the Archives stop. I walked the rest of the way to the Gallery in the cloudless sapphire sky. Regardless of the problems swirling like the ruby leaves around me, the exciting fall weather infused me with joy. I hoped the director wouldn't blow a fuse when he found out I paid a visit to the plaintiffs suing us. But since I was delivering good news, relatively speaking, I figured he would forgive me for not running it by him first. The fact that David had gone with me fortified my courage.

I took the power steps up the white staircase to the director's office.

"You what?" John's response was stronger than I had anticipated.

"David and I called on Colette and Jacques Alexander and got them to agree to tell their lawyer, whom they have never met by the way, to delay the lawsuit. I know it's unorthodox."

"You were lucky. Go report your trip to Legal. They're not going to be happy."

"But they will be happy to receive these," I handed John the documents Jacques Alexander had given me showing *Lady in Waiting's* history of ownership.

John shook his head. "Millicent. You're a risk taker. So far it has paid off for you."

I skipped down the white staircase, grinning.

I called Lee to give her an update on my visits in Paris and Jerusalem.

"Millie, do you know how much longer it's going to take before an agreement is reached on the painting?" Lee's voiced sounded strained.

"I wish I knew. They are moving as fast as they can. David Perry, the art historian from California, is trying to figure out the code with a former colleague at the National Security Agency. Paul Morton, the Gallery's Vermeer expert, is still examining the painting to determine if it's a real Vermeer. That's where we are. Is the I.R.S. putting pressure on you?"

"Terribly."

"Do they know you might have a Vermeer that will change your situation dramatically?"

"I don't think they give a damn, frankly. They want the money."

"Who is your agent? I wonder if I could talk to him or her."

"Let me look that up and I'll call you," Lee said, her voice weary.

"Lee, try not to worry. I know that's sounds ridiculous for me to say. But I will find a way out of this. I hate to see you so upset."

"Thanks, darling. Things will work out. For better or worse. They always do."

It was the 'for worse' I was worried about. I saw another call coming in.

"Hey, Millicent, how was Paris?" Phillip's voice sounded more upbeat than ever.

"Paris was *tres bien*."

"So what'd you do?"

"I called on the Alexander heirs, grandchildren of the couple whose painting ended up at Lee Trevor's home."

"Yeah, I know that. Besides that."

"Went to dinner. Saw the Eiffel Tower. The usual stuff."

"With that guy."

"Yes, with David Perry from California."

"Is he married?"

"What is this, twenty questions?" I couldn't believe Phillip's newfound interest in my life.

"Why don't you come to Dallas? It's not Paris but we've got a few choice spots." I nearly fell out of my chair. Phillip had never invited me to Dallas before.

"When are you thinking?" popped out of my mouth.

"This Saturday. A friend of mine has a plane and can give you a lift."

"Sounds fun," I said flatly. "Let me double check my calendar, Phillip. I want to make sure I haven't promised something I'm forgetting." I had been waiting for months for Phillip to take the lead. Now I didn't care.

"A break would do you good. Anyway, you can't solve Lee's problems or solve the secret code." Phillip said in his flippant way.

I hated the sound of Phillip's tone of voice. He had a way of dismissing me and what ever issues I was dealing with. The only thing he didn't say was 'don't worry your pretty little head about it.' All of a sudden, I wanted to do both. Solve Lee's tax problems and solve the secret code.

"I'll call you," I told him. No more designer doormat.

"Hurry and let me know. I need to make my plans."

Was Phillip always this myopic and I was only now beginning to notice?

Caroline Higgins-McNiece's Bing-cherry bob and red glasses appeared in my office doorway.

"Millicent, how much do you know about Theodore Pennington?"

"Not that much. I was in his Boston apartment. Appears to be well situated. Seems to know a good bit about art."

"Well, you know I've been checking into the

provenance of his so-called Matisse. We can't find a thing on it. In fact, it has some features that are very suspicious. Forgery suspicious. The X-ray is too clean. Usually we find corrections in the composition, underdrawings. Something doesn't smell right," Caroline concluded.

"You're kidding," I exhaled.

"I wish I were."

"This is awkward. What next?" I asked.

"We ask the donor to take back the piece. We can't accept it," she said.

"I guess I get to make that call," I muttered.

"Afraid so." Caroline shrugged and left.

I glanced at the many art books lining my bookcase. I pulled out the one on Henri Matisse and flipped through it. Would these be easy to forge? I turned to my computer and entered Matisse's *Sleeping Woman* on the National Gallery's website. The exact title is *Still Life with Sleeping Woman*. The image bore a striking resemblance to the fake Matisse that Theodore Pennington tried to give the Gallery. It had been confiscated in 1941 by the ERR, the notorious Nazi agency.

I continued reading the provenance. It also was snatched by Hermann Goering from the Jeu de Paume. But only to trade it. So Theo knew the history of the real painting and used the story to distract us from his fake painting? Surely he knew the National Gallery of Art would figure this out. What was his real motive? Well, in any case I might as well get this over. I punched in

Theodore Pennington's number.

"Theo, this is Millicent Clermont at the National Gallery."

"Yes, Millicent, how nice to hear from you."

"I'm afraid I have some disappointing news."

"You don't say."

"I hate to tell you this, but the Gallery cannot accept your painting."

"Why not? It's a fine painting."

"Our researchers can't find any provenance entries for it. It's as if it was created out of thin air."

"Now wait just a minute, young lady. What are you implying? I'll have you know that my mother was an expert in art."

"I'm sure she was. The Gallery has very high standards and ..."

"Well, in that case," he said in a huff, "I'll come get it. And tell those little twits in your paint-by-number restoration shop, they don't know what the fuck they're talking about." With that, he slammed down the phone.

24

National Gallery of Art
Washington D.C.

The next day I got a call from Caroline.

"Millie, Theodore Pennington is on his way to Conservation."

I ran to the West Building and let myself in through the unmarked doors.

Theo never said a word to me nor ever made direct eye contact. He was friendly to Caroline at first. Strange but friendly. He didn't want to discuss his painting at all. He wanted Caroline to show him what else they were working on. Once he saw the painting from Whittington, that's all he was interested in. He tried to act casual, but if eyes had mouths, he would have eaten the canvas.

"Have you taken X-rays of it?" he wanted to know.

"Yes, we have," Caroline told him.

"May I see them?"

"I'm not at liberty to do that, Mr. Pennington," Caroline explained.

"You bloody paint-by-number restorer!" Theo got so red in the face I thought he would have a heart attack. "You and your crew are two-bit imposters!"

"Talk about the pot calling the kettle black," Caroline said.

"Fuck you! You don't deserve my painting." The rumpled man grabbed his so-called Matisse and stormed out.

"Caroline, I'm so sorry. I thought the English were prim and proper."

"I'm not sure he has a drop of English blood in him. Something's not cricket with him. If I were to bet, that painting he brought in is as fake as a Chinese Rolex."

"But why would he go to all that trouble? And why would he say the painting had been in Goering's control?"

"To throw us off. People do weird things. And in the art world, multiply that by a million."

"I guess if he didn't actually sell the painting, he didn't commit a crime."

"It's fraudulent to knowingly offer a painting that's a forgery whether you are giving it away or selling it."

"Is this something the Gallery would turn over to law enforcement?"

"It's not worth the publicity."

My intra office phone rang. "Miss Clermont, you've got a beautiful bouquet of flowers down here," the guard at the security desk said.

"Gosh, that doesn't happen often. Thanks, Mike. I'll be right down." I took the elevator to the first floor and spotted a gorgeous arrangement. I looked at the card: "Come to Dallas, Love, Phillip." Why is Phillip interested now that I care less about him?

David would be at my house in a couple of minutes. I lit the jasmine candle and checked my makeup in the front mirror. I jumped when the doorbell rang.

He put his briefcase down and hugged me. I felt whole.

"We're at a standstill on the code." David scanned my face.

I put my finger to my lips and pulled David toward the kitchen.

"Let me fix some tea." I closed the French doors between the living room and kitchen. "Haywood got a tip that someone bugged the mantle. The guys didn't find anything but I don't feel safe in that room."

David nodded and opened his briefcase, pulled out his papers, and spread them on the kitchen island. He looked at the code: NSIM 880099.

I handed David a cup of hot tea.

"Did Haywood talk to Otto Baader?" David asked.

"He won't talk. Haywood doesn't think Baader knows what the code means. But he's desperate to get his hands on it."

I was standing on the other side of my kitchen island

and could see the X-ray of the painting showing the code in the overpainting. Upside down, it read "660088 WISN." I suddenly knew that that was the right way to read the code.

"David, did Patrick run the code upside down?" I turned the X-ray photo around so David could read it that way.

He looked intently at the numbers and letters. "Millicent, you clever woman, you."

He picked up his safe cell phone.

"Patrick, I'm embarrassed that I didn't think of this, but Millie read the code upside down and wondered if we had examined it that way.... Yeah, you'd think we would have figured that out with fifty years of experience between us. Okay, call me back."

In a few minutes, David's secure phone rang. "The WISM stands for Wiesen? There are three towns named Wiesen? Thanks, Patrick. I'll Google it." David's pleased expression spread across his handsome face. "Millicent, I owe you."

"What did he say?"

"Patrick agrees that the code might point to the hiding place of stolen art and he thinks it's in Wiesen."

I sat down on the nearest barstool. "What's the next step?"

"Figure out which town of Wiesen the code refers to and book a flight as soon as possible. We'll have to hurry."

"David, I can't go. I am so far behind at work and frankly, I can't afford it." My cell phone rang. "Hi, Haywood."

"Millicent, our source meant to tell us the bug is in the mantle of the baby house."

"Baby house? You mean my dollhouse?" My eyes were on stems as I looked at David and then at the dollhouse right in front of us in my breakfast room. "I'll call you back."

I peered into the living room of my dollhouse. I then remembered putting back a picture that had fallen in the miniature room when I was showing David the dollhouse earlier. I carefully removed the tiny mantle and when I did, a small round device fell off. This tiny device had transmitted every word David and I had just spoken about the secret code.

David and I moved upstairs with his computer and closed the door to my bedroom.

"Are you sure it's safe up here?" I asked.

David shook his head. "We need to move fast." He peered at his computer screen. "There's not much in Wiesen, Austria besides a jazz festival in the summer. However, Hitler was from Linz, Austria. Remember, he was going to build a world class museum in Linz."

"Yeah, using all the art he stole," I added.

"Hitler felt entitled as victor. In fact, the entitlement of conquerors goes clear back to the Bible." David rubbed his eyes and then clicked his computer keys. "Wiesen, Switzerland is even smaller. I'm thinking Wiesen, Germany might be the place."

"Based on what?"

"A hunch."

"What's it close to?" I had never been to Germany and had no interest in going.

"It's not far from Frankfort. Here it is. Wiesen, Bavaria. Come look at this satellite shot. It even has a street called Wiesen. It's so small that it would have been easy for the Monuments Men to miss it."

"The Monuments Men?"

David turned from his computer screen. "In 1943, President Roosevelt approved what was officially called the Monuments, Fine Arts, and Archives program, or MFAA. It was a group of young museum directors and curators, art professors and architects who volunteered to help identify and protect priceless monuments and other art treasures. And they weren't all men, there were some women in the group too. They gave maps to American pilots so they could avoid bombing culturally important buildings.

"As the Allied Forces moved into France and Germany toward the end of the war, their mission shifted from protecting the art to finding the massive amount of stolen art. The Nazis hid what they had confiscated in castles, churches, and caves. The largest discovery was in the Alt Aussee salt mine in Austria. They found over 6,500 paintings and thousands of pieces of sculpture including a sculpture by Michelangelo and two paintings by Vermeer all meant for Hitler's new museum."

"Wow. Unbelievable. Which Vermeer paintings?"

"*The Art of Painting* and *The Astronomer*. Both are great works, but I particularly like *The Art of Painting*. It shows a woman wearing a laurel wreath signifying honor and glory. She holds a large book and trumpet, signifying Clio, the muse of history. An artist in the foreground is painting her. He is dressed not as a common painter but in a stylish doublet, as an aristocrat. Some think it is Vermeer himself. Vermeer held onto *The Art of Painting* until his death in 1675. Vermeer's widow tried to keep it but was forced to sell it.

"Then in the thirties it was rumored that Andrew Mellon was interested in purchasing the painting from an Austrian family, but he died in 1937. By 1938 Germany had annexed Austria so that sale, even if it was on the table, would have been cancelled. It now hangs in the Kunsthistorisches Museum in Vienna."

"Gosh, what a history," I said.

"Sorry I fall into lecture mode at the drop of a hat." David turned back to the computer screen.

"No, really, I love listening to you. And I would give anything if I could go with you, David. But really I can't."

David looked straight at me. "I'll take care of the expenses. And if you want, I'll talk to John Peale."

The offer of covering the costs was tempting. But I

wasn't about to have a man, even David, step in for me. "No, that's okay. I'll handle it."

My climb up the white power steps to the director's office took more energy than I had. Nothing ventured, nothing gained. I proceeded into John's office.

"Now you want to go to Wiesen, Germany?" the director's voice boomed. "That's not within the purview of your job, Millicent. It won't bring a dime into the Gallery. Your trip to Paris and Jerusalem turned out okay but Legal went crazy. Remember your job is to raise money."

"John, in all due respect I have a feeling something big is waiting for us."

"If I said that to Secretary Clinton or Chief Justice Roberts and the other trustees I report to, they would laugh me out of the room," John Peale said only slightly less angry.

"But you won't prevent me from going," I looked at my boss earnestly. I was really out on a limb now.

"It's your business what you do in your personal life as long as you don't reflect poorly on the Gallery." John looked down at his desk and picked up his pen. Meeting over.

"I'll be back next week." I turned, bowing, and exited.

25

Wiesen, Germany

I grinned when David pulled up in front of baggage claim at the Frankfort Airport in a rented Volkswagen, 'the people's car' designed by Ferdinand Porsche and his son per Hitler's direction.

We were soon on our way to Wiesen, the tiny Bavarian town set in the rolling hills of Germany. Population: 1,000. As we drove east, I was surprised at what I saw. Germany wasn't as ugly as I thought it would be. Actually it was quite beautiful. Within an hour we entered the tiny village of Wiesen.

"660088" David read from his notes. We looked at every street address. Nothing remotely resembled these numbers. The town was so small the Internet had not been much help.

"David! That street sign says Wiesen!" I pointed as we drove past.

He swung the bug around and turned onto the narrow street. We saw only single digit addresses.

"Let's ask someone." I proposed.

"No. I'll figure it out."

We drove up and down the winding street. Nothing with the numbers in the secret code. In fact only a few buildings had any kind of address.

"Let's get a drink. Look at that little place." I pointed to a quaint restaurant. David parked the blue bug on the street and we entered the bierlokal. The place reeked of bratwurst. David ordered beer in German. He chose Schneider Wiesen Edel-Weisse to be in theme.

"Das gut." David licked his lips.

The healthy waitress with red cheeks delivered our check with an English, "Thank you for coming."

"Fraulein, we are looking for an address but can't seem to find it," David said politely as he showed her the numbers 660088.

"Ja. Our mail code is 60088."

"Are there addresses with single numbers?"

"Ja. We are number 3 Wiesen. Next door is the butcher, he's number five. Maybe the church across the way?"

We finished our beer, left money on the table, and were outside in a matter of minutes.

The church across the street was beautiful red brick with limestone trim in a Romanesque style. We read the sign: St. Michael's Cathedral. A stone paver next to it said in faint lettering: Six Wiesen. David tested the middle door of the three-portal entrance. It was open.

"How gorgeous," I said admiring the light blue, gold, and creamy-white colors.

"Classic Bavarian baroque interior," David said as he peered up at the five altars. "See the middle statue? That's St. Michael standing in conquest of the fallen angels."

I was not Catholic but certainly appreciated their elaborate places of worship. We were the only ones in the sanctuary. The cool, quiet space was calming.

A priest in long black garb appeared out of nowhere. "May I help you?" he said in English with a strong German accent as he dry washed his hands. He wore a heavy gold cross, encrusted with precious stones.

"Oh, hello," David said. "We're art historians on tour. This is a beautiful church. Quite a magnificent structure for such a small town."

"We are fortunate to have generous benefactors to support God's work. The cornerstone was laid in 1860. Pope Pius IX blessed the statue of St. Michael in 1865 which may be the reason it has survived all these years."

"Are there other parts of the church we might see?" David asked.

"This main section is open to the public. The other areas are makeshift living quarters for the sisters and priests who serve the parish."

"Was the church used during World War II in any way?"

"I'm sorry. You will have to pardon me. I have a prior

appointment for which I cannot be late. I will show you out." The black robed man gestured toward the main entrance. His hands were delicate. No hard work there.

"Is the church open every day?" I asked.

"Generally, yes. But we will be closing tomorrow for much needed repairs." The priest reminded me of Ewan McGregor in *Angels and Demons.*

We stood on the front steps in the bright sun. "He sure clammed up when you asked about World War II," I said as I blocked the sun with my hand.

"Nazis were protected by some Catholic churches, and confiscated art has been found in more than one. His behavior makes me think St. Michael's was one of them."

"But how can we find out? Don't tell me you're an undercover agent too."

"No, but I have a plan."

In our modest room in the only hotel in town, the family-run Landgasthof Berghorf, I smeared my mascara, flatted my hair—the worst part—and donned the old clothes we had bought at a flea market. After it turned dark, we left the hotel wearing our indigent disguises. We approached the back of the church. David surveyed the exterior looking for doors, passageways, anything that might lead to underground storage. If someone caught us, we would act as if we were trying to get a food hand out from the sisters or a warm place to stay the night.

David came across a latched door on the side of the

church. In no time he had it open. Great. David wasn't an art historian; he was a burglar. "Come on," he whispered.

We walked down a dimly lit corridor, dank and musty smelling, which turned sharply to the left. The odor of old earth became stronger as the light diminished. Another turn and we saw a thin white line at floor level, light coming through a closed door. David turned to me and put his index finger to his mouth. I couldn't have uttered an audible sound if I had wanted to.

David quickly stepped forward and threw his weight against the door. Since the door wasn't locked, he sailed into the room full of crates and paintings. A man was examining a small painting, his foggy wire glasses askew on his puffy face.

"Theodore Pennington!" I exclaimed. "What are you doing here?"

"What the hell?" Theo dropped the painting he had been holding.

David looked at me surprised. "You know this guy?"

Theodore's round face was flushed crimson.

"Yes, he tried to give the Gallery a Matisse. A fake Matisse," I said.

"Well, Ms. Clermont," Theo pronounced as he raised a handgun to our faces. "It's too bad you are here."

David's hand went out to protect me as we both stepped back.

"There's plenty of art here for us to divide," David said in a measured tone.

"Divide? Don't think for a moment I'm going to give up anything from my father's treasure trove."

"Your father? Who was your father?

"My father was the great General Wilhelm Baader. He should have refused the underarm tattoo showing his blood type like Dr. Mengele did. His tattoo did him in. I don't mind telling you since you won't be leaving here alive."

And here I thought Theodore Pennington was a Boston Brahmin. "You're the brother of Otto Baader?" I was so confounded I lost my fear.

"Yes. My name is Max Baader. My mother was English, married to a German Jew. She had an affair with my father to try to save her husband. Pity it didn't work."

"All this art was stolen by your father during the war?" David looked at the many paintings propped against the walls. Old Masters, religious art, portraits, and landscapes large and small.

"That's why they call it the spoils of war." Max said.

"But it doesn't belong to you," David said.

"Of course it does. I am in possession. And you are nothing but common burglars." He leveled the gun at us.

"Calm down, Mr. Baader, whatever your name is," David said. "I'm sure we can come up with a suitable solution."

"There is only one solution, my friends," the man with the gun said.

With a sudden motion, David upturned a crate in

front of Max. The gun went off as Max fell backward. David grabbed my hand and pulled me out of the room and down the dark hall. We ran quickly, turned the corner, and bumped head on into the priest we had seen earlier.

Before we knew what had happened, we were covered in black cloth. I was shoved against David, cutting my lip. Then something constricted the cloth making it impossible to move.

"You should never have come here." We heard the muffled voice of the priest. "It leaves us with no alternative."

David and I were in complete darkness as we were led step by awkward step in our captor's black robe.

"Ouch!" I said after David stepped on my toe.

"Sorry." He grabbed my hand and squeezed it.

We were shoved and fell down on top of one another on a cold stone floor.

"No one will ever find you now," the priest said. We heard a door slammed shut.

We waited for a few minutes but heard nothing. We wiggled out of our heavy cloth prison. The room was pitch black but I began to make out David's face. He spread out the cloth so we could sit on it. Compared to the chilling damp stone, the rough wool felt downright luxurious. If I were going to die, at least I would not leave this earth alone. I was with the person I loved. Maybe I should tell him before they killed us.

"Breathe." David instructed me.

"Breathe?"

"Yes, take measured breaths. It will calm your body and put you in touch with the breath of God."

"That's good. Because I think we'll be visiting Him very soon," I half-jokingly said.

"Don't worry, Millicent. Stay in the spirit. We'll figure out an escape plan."

"I'm glad you're so positive."

"Breathe," he reminded me.

"At least we have our cell phones." I took mine out and looked at the reception bars. Nothing.

"Even if we could get a signal I don't know who we would call. The locals would believe the priest over some bums who broke into the town church."

I shivered and hugged my knees. David put his arm around me. The priest had said the church was going to be closed tomorrow. No telling how long we were going to be here. I dozed off next to David's warm body.

A loud explosion woke me up. I looked at David in the inky light. We heard footsteps stomping through the passageways. Oh, no. This was it. My breath was shallow and quick. David stood in front of the door listening.

We could hear faint voices but couldn't make out what was being said. They grew louder but still we couldn't understand the words.

Then I heard my name.

"Millicent?" The muffled voice said.

I stood up.

"David?" said the same voice.

David banged on the door. "We're in here!"

"Stand back. We'll have to fire through the lock."

A swift shot whistled, splintering the door.

Who should come through the door, but two men in black, and Haywood, my favorite bi-polar nutcase.

"Haywood! Thank God!" I was in tears as I hugged him.

"You guys all right?" Haywood held me by the shoulders, and then looked at David, smiling.

"We're great now," David said.

"Millicent, once again you have helped us nab our man. And you have led us to a treasure trove of Nazi looted art. Maybe you should consider a career with the F.B.I."

"Yeah, right." I rolled my eyes. "Sign me up."

"How'd you find us?" David asked.

"We tracked your cell phone signals."

David nodded.

"Did you get Theodore Pennington?" I asked.

"You mean Max Baader," Haywood answered. "INTERPOL has him in custody. Max sure has a mouth on him."

"And the art?" David looked from Haywood to the other agents.

"All of it is being inventoried as we speak," Haywood said, obviously pleased with the outcome. "INTERPOL will secure the necessary releases from the German government and then it will be shipped to Paris. A lot of folks are going to be happy once their art is returned to them. Meanwhile, you guys need to get cleaned up. You look like a couple of bums."

Part Three

"Love is the extremely difficult realization that something other than oneself is real. Love, and so art and morals, is the discovery of reality."
Iris Murdoch

26

Washington D.C.

Haywood, David, and I flew back to New York's JFK Airport, celebrating all the way. I would hate myself later for the champagne puff on my body, but I could not have been happier. We were heroes. And I was with the man of my dreams.

As the flight attendant poured our third glass, David, ever the historian, asked, "Do you know what the champagne bottle was used for besides this bubbly drink?"

I raised my eyebrows at another display of David's encyclopedic brain. "No. Do tell."

"Napoleon's biggest challenge was how to feed his enormous army," David began. "While pondering over his favorite glass of champagne, Napoleon decided to offer prize money to the person who invented a way to feed his hungry soldiers. In 1810, an ex-chef and bottle-washer, Nicolas Appert, won for his idea of putting food in a bottle, sealing, heating, and cooling it. Champagne bottles were plentiful in France. So Napoleon's armies soon began eating vegetable soup and beef stew out of champagne bottles."

"I'll drink to that." Haywood raised his glass.

Between the champagne and the emotional highs of the trip, I couldn't keep my eyes open, and bed head or not, I fell fast sleep.

Arriving at JFK, we lugged ourselves off the plane. David needed to get back to San Diego. We hugged, we kissed, and confirmed my trip to see him on the West coast. Haywood and I headed to D.C.

As soon as I got home, I called my mother and then Lee Trevor.

"You're not going to believe this but the secret code in your painting has unearthed several missing paintings and sculpture that have been hidden in Germany since the war, in a church no less."

"How extraordinary, Millie. I'm glad some good has come from all of this. Any news on my painting?"

"I'll call the Gallery as soon as we hang up. But once I find out the status, I'll call you. And I'm going to go see someone at the I.R.S."

"The sooner the better."

"I'm so sorry it has taken so long. But this latest discovery will help take the heat off."

"Tell that to the I.R.S."

"Lee, something else has happened."

"I can't take any more bad news."

"Oh, it's not bad at all. I'm in love with David Perry."

"David Perry?"

"The art historian from San Diego. The one I've been with in Germany."

"Sorry I've been too wrapped up in my own problems. I'd love to meet him, Millie. When can you come to Whittington?"

"David had to get back to California. The next time he's on the East Coast, I'll let you know. I think you'll be impressed with him."

"If you are, darling, I know I will be."

"Try not to worry, Lee. Everything should be resolved soon."

"Call me as soon as you hear anything," Lee's depressed voice faded as she hung up.

I hopped up the white stairs to the director's office.

"You and David make quite a team," John said.

I beamed from head to toe.

"And you certainly are our most interesting development officer." John shook his head. "Part fundraiser, part volunteer F.B.I. agent."

"I didn't think my job would entail rubbing shoulders with the sons of a Nazi general."

"I'm proud of your work. It will take several weeks to verify all the pieces found in Germany. But what we know already is a bonanza for the art world as well as the rightful owners."

"Development is much more exciting than I thought it would be."

"It's usually not *this* exciting."

"Has Paul made a determination about *Lady in Waiting*? Is it a real Vermeer?"

"Paul is still studying it and conferring with other curators, but he should be releasing his findings soon."

"You know, Mrs. Trevor is quite anxious."

"Authentication of a painting as important as this cannot be rushed," John said, concluding our meeting.

Paul met me in the Conservation Department. Caroline had displayed the films of *Lady in Waiting* on the light board. It was like looking at an X-ray of a person except instead outlines of bone and organs, images in the painting—the woman's dress, objects in the room, and overall composition— showed up in varying degrees of white and gray. Some images were more pronounced than others based on the particular pigment used. Paints with high lead content showed up white in the slick black sheet.

"Here are the infrared reflectogram results," Caroline said as she attached another set of films to the lighted panel.

"What are these other lines and images? I guess the artist changed his mind," I said. "Here's a dog that's not in the finished painting."

"Exactly," Paul countered. "In fact that is one of the

indicators that a painting is authentic. The number of pentimenti is higher in Old Masters. Forgers forget this and produce paintings without the added images. This one from Whittington doesn't have as much pentimenti one would expect in a Vermeer."

"But that doesn't mean it isn't?" My face felt hot.

"I can't really say one way or another at this point," Paul said.

"If a forger paints a great painting, why do we care if it's not what we thought it was? Why does it matter? If the technique, composition, and overall aesthetics are there?" I desperately wanted Lee's painting to be a Vermeer.

"Actually human beings care deeply whether a work of art is authentic," Paul said. "When Goering found out the painting he bought was in fact a forgery by Van Meegeren, he went into a rage. People relate to objects around them according to their history as well as their physical and artistic properties. A painting created purposely to dupe the buyer makes the buyer feel cheated. It's the existential issue of what is real and what is fake. Everyone desperately seeks the authentic over the illusionary, even an individual who otherwise violates all rules of decency and integrity."

"So, Paul.... when do you think you will conclude your findings?"

"We're waiting on a few more tests to come back. And we have an outside consultant coming in to look at the fingerprints we found."

"Fingerprints on the painting? Whose?" I asked, baffled.

"Possibly Vermeer's fingerprints. I don't put any credence in this sort of so-called scientific authentication but one of our other curators wants to examine this angle," Paul said. "Museums and curators can destroy their credibility if an authentication turns out to be wrong. Abraham Bredius was considered the greatest expert on Dutch paintings before World War II. He ruined his reputation after declaring *Christ and the Disciplines at Emmaus* to be a Vermeer when in fact it was a Han van Meegeren forgery."

"How long will this take?"

"Don't know. The fingerprint expert is on her way over," Paul answered.

"While I'm here, would you show me what you found?"

"Sure," Paul said finding his horn-rimmed glasses in his pocket and putting them on. "See this right here." Paul pointed to a barely discernible pattern. "This is a visible print."

"As opposed to an invisible print?"

"As opposed to a latent print. A latent print is a fingerprint made by sweat and has to be dusted or otherwise made visible using a chemical process. A visible print is one where the finger has left a mark either in wet paint or with ink."

"I've never heard of this. How long has fingerprint

authentication been around?"

"The issue surfaced in a 1920s newspaper article on a Kansas case regarding a Leonardo di Vinci portrait. But it wasn't until 1994 that the first *official*," Paul made quotation marks with his fingers, "fingerprint attribution was declared concerning a J.M.W. Turner painting. In 2009 another portrait by Leonardo di Vinci was in the news based on a fingerprint match with a di Vinci painting in the Vatican. Again, I believe in the traditional method of studying an artist's work for years and then as in this case, using the results of X-rays, infrared reflectograms, and other well-known technical examinations to form an opinion. It's a combination of scientific data and intuition. The intuition part of it is called connoisseurship, when a person can look at a work of art and have an immediate sense that is authentic."

"So what is your immediate sense of this painting?" I asked afraid of his answer.

Paul took off his glasses. "I really can't say yet."

27

The Internal Revenue Service
Washington, D.C.

The I.R.S. headquarters, a plain gray building on Constitution Avenue, sent the message "no joking allowed." Everyone I saw resembled the building: humorless. The general counsel was a surprise.

The head of the legal department, Johnson Milbank, was an engaging gentleman, reminding me of an English nobleman rather than one of the toughest government officials in Washington. My Google search revealed he had graduated from Harvard University, summa cum laude. Further sites indicated he was related to everyone who had ever had a hand in founding this country, a member of The First Families of Mississippi, the Cincinnati Club, and every other elite club known to man. Unlike some powerful and brilliant men, Johnson Milbank's manners equaled his intelligence and status.

"Ms. Clermont, how can I help?" Johnson Milbank motioned to a Chippendale chair. "Please be seated."

If tea and scones were rolled out on a two-tiered butler tray, I would not have been surprised.

"Mr. Milbank, thank you for seeing me. As I mentioned on the phone, I am here to discuss Mrs. Lee Trevor of Whittington Plantation. Mrs. Trevor's husband acquired a fine Dutch painting in the sixties that is on the list of Nazi looted art. An art restitution lawyer discovered this a few weeks ago. Meanwhile, Mrs. Trevor received an enormous tax bill related to her deceased husband's business dealings she knew nothing about. Mrs. Trevor is going to give the painting, which is likely a painting by Johannes Vermeer, to the National Gallery of Art.

"I am here to ask you, to plead with you, to consider giving Mrs. Trevor a tax credit instead of a tax deduction for her gift to the Gallery. And after all, her gift is going to the United States government. Mrs. Trevor doesn't receive much income, so a tax deduction would not help her." I felt my whole future depended on Johnson Milbank's answer. And I knew I had to remain silent. I stopped my jiggling foot.

His fingers touched each other, a spider on a mirror. His brow furrowed. I looked at his black glasses wondering how many years ago he had bought his vintage frames.

"Ms. Clermont, this is highly unusual. Not something the I.R.S. generally does. I don't know if you studied Emmanuel Kant and the Categorical Imperative. The Categorical Imperative asks us to base our actions on the hypothesis that everyone could do the same and it would be good for society. What if we gave everyone a tax credit for giving art to the National Gallery? Do you know what that would mean for our government?"

"Yes, I studied philosophy and I know about Kant's Categorical Imperative. But, Mr. Milbank, this is an extraordinary case. Through the gift to the Gallery, the citizens of the United States will gain one of the most valuable works of art that ever existed."

More furrowed brow. More spider-on-the mirror fingers.

"Ms. Clermont, given these unusual circumstances, this is a matter that the I.R.S. can take under advisement. It takes time for any decision to be processed through our bureaucratic maze, but I think this case might be given consideration."

"So, that's a yes? A maybe? But definitely not a no?"

"Yes. One of those outcomes."

28

San Diego

David picked me up at the airport in an old tan S.U.V., a Chevrolet or something. I didn't think he would ever understand my Neiman Marcus bills. We drove past the San Diego bay filled with ships and yachts, heading north to the small community of Rancho Santa Fe for lunch at Delicias Restaurant.

"Originally Rancho Santa Fe was part of an 1830 Spanish land grant to the Santa Fe Railroad," David said as the waiter poured me a glass of Chardonnay. "In the 1920s, the railroad company hired a female architect by the name of Lilian Rice to design the town. Her office was right over there on the corner of Paseo Delicias and La Granada. She was one of the first women to graduate from the University of California in 1910."

I admired the Spanish Colonial architecture: terra cotta tiled roofs over creamy white adobe buildings. Patios and courtyards dressed with black grillwork like Spanish women wearing black lace mantillas. Voluminous hot pink flowers caught my eye. Jasmine infused my nose. I could understand how one could get used to this. Sitting outside this time of year was impossible in Washington.

"The Crab Sourdough Panini with Truffle Fries is very good," David said.

After our white wine buzz, delicious sandwich, and the best French fries I had ever eaten, we arrived at David's home, two minutes away. Lush greenery gave way to a heavy carved door that opened into a spacious house of windows and art.

"David, how gorgeous. And what an art collection." I scanned the room to see if I could identify his eclectic mix. Miró, Chagall, Turner, O'Keefe.

"The best way to become good at art history is to live with the subject."

I was sinking deeper and deeper into this man. Good that we lived on opposite coasts.

"I love these flowers." I walked over to the dining room table to sniff the blue hydrangeas and pale pink peonies.

"The tints of morning and evening."

I gave him a quizzical look.

"It's from my favorite Thoreau poem. 'The true harvest of my daily life is as indescribable as the tints of morning and evening.'"

"That's beautiful."

"I thought you'd prefer the guest room and bath for dressing," he said as he dropped my luggage in the charming bedroom. I wondered if his late wife had decorated this room. I felt like 'the other woman' even though his wife was dead. But not her presence in the house.

"Let's go for a quick jog. It's a perfect way to see the neighborhood."

"I'll be ready in five minutes."

We jogged past house after house with beautiful gardens. This was a glorious place with perfect seventy-degree weather.

"David, did you grow up here in Rancho Santa Fe?"

"No. I grew up outside of San Francisco. I moved here ten years ago. My house was a complete redo. It had no air conditioning, no pool, really wasn't much. A lot of the remodel I did myself. I enjoy carpentry and painting. Working on the house is therapy too."

David bore the marks of his wife's death still.

"Your art collection is amazing," I said, stopping to catch my breath. "Were your parents art collectors?"

"They appreciated it but never owned any. I started buying art when I was in college and then kept trading up. Some men play golf, buy cars and boats; I love art. For one thing, it usually appreciates over time. And paintings are a great way to learn history and social mores."

We circled around the golf course and headed back to his house. This man had impressive values.

"Tonight we should have about fifty people here. I

told my friends they need to think about giving five thousand each to the National Gallery. Well, each couple."

"David. Gosh, thank you."

That evening I put on my pale green Nicole Miller dress, my black Christian Louboutin heels with the red soles, no stockings, black designer earrings, no necklace, matching cuff bracelets. I felt like a princess. David was magnanimous when he introduced me to his friends—doctors, professors, lawyers, artists.

"Thank you all for coming," I began. "Thank you, David, for hosting this event." I beamed at David and he beamed back. "Rancho Santa Fe is an incredibly beautiful place and I can understand how you might never want to leave. But I promise you, when you come to the National Gallery of Art in Washington, D.C., I will give you an insider experience of one of the most magnificent museums in the world. We can trace, through the museum's art, the history of humankind from the beginning of civilization up to the present moment. We can gaze upon Ginevra de' Benci, the only Leonardo da Vinci painting to live permanently in the Western hemisphere. We can ponder the meaning of our vast Modern and Contemporary Collections housed in I.M. Pei's stunning East Building. We would marvel at Rembrandts and Vermeers in John Russell Pope's majestic West Building. There is something for everyone, and it is truly a gift to the nation, made possible by Andrew Mellon and perpetuated by generous donors. Maybe you will become one of those fortunate people who support our greatest treasures. Thank you."

David led the applause and then handed me a glass of champagne.

"You were terrific," he whispered in my ear. "I'm so proud to be with you."

As the evening wrapped up, each couple left an envelope on the foyer table.

With everyone gone, we sat in the living room with our feet up. David had me open each envelope. A five thousand check, another five thousand check, a ten thousand check, on and on, then a twenty-five thousand check. The evening's total came to a hundred and seventy-five thousand dollars. That would take some of the pressure off. Then David took my hand and led me to his bedroom.

"I wish you could stay longer," David said as we drove to the airport Sunday morning.

"I do too. It was a perfect weekend. Thank you for everything. Your friends are great. And of course I love them for giving to the Gallery."

David took my bag out of the back of his car and gave it to the skycap. "Thank you for coming, Millicent," he said as he held me close.

"You know, you can call me Millie."

"I will if you want me to, but I love the name

Millicent."

"Fine, whatever. Just call me."

We kissed and hugged one more time and I waved goodbye with my heart filled with flowers. Finally my luck in love had changed.

29
Washington, D.C.

Rather than take the Metro, I drove to the Gallery praying I could find a parking space on the Mall in the only two blocks that didn't have parking meters. I thanked my parking guardian angel as I parallel parked at 4th and Madison.

Once at my desk, I decided to check out the Gallery's website. I couldn't make Paul Morton go faster in authenticating the painting. And I couldn't make the I.R.S. speed up. I opened up nga.gov and entered one of my favorite paintings, *Calvary* by the Master of the Death of Saint Nicolas of Münster circa 1470-80. The image popped up with menu items such as the location in the museum and its provenance.

Calvary was a large painting with the traditional crucifixion scene, Jesus in the middle flanked by a criminal on each side. Tiny angels held chalices close to Jesus' body to catch his blood. The thief on Jesus' right had a miniature demon taking his soul, represented as a minuscule person, to hell. The thief on Jesus' left had a tiny angel taking his soul, also represented by a minuscule person, to heaven. It wasn't only my love of miniatures that captivated me. The artist's delightful way of showing good and evil, heaven and hell, and the journey of the soul after death was unique.

The unknown artist who painted this magnificent work was referred to as 'Master of' because the work was similar in style to *The Death of Saint Nicolas of Münster*, hence the attribution 'Master of.'

Looking up the provenance of *Calvary* on the NGA website shocked me. In July 1940, Nazis confiscated the painting from André Seligmann and took it to the German Embassy in Paris. From there it was taken to the Jeu de Paume. Then Hermann Goering took it from the Jeu de Paume for his own personal use on November 5, 1940. How many other paintings that I admired had been kidnapped by the Nazis?

Fortunately, the Allies recovered *Calvary* on October 30, 1946 and restituted it to France. It lived at the Louvre from 1951 until 1999 when it was returned to the daughters of André Seligmann. The National Gallery purchased it June 6, 2000. At least this one had a happy ending. Would there be a happy ending for *Lady in Waiting*?

My cell phone rang. I almost tripped over myself trying to get to it in my purse. I could see it was David on caller ID. It had been an entire week since I returned from

San Diego. I hadn't heard one peep from him.

"Millicent, hi," David voice was low and listless.

"Is something wrong, David? You sound different."

"It's the anniversary of my wife's death. I still have a hard time pretending this day doesn't matter."

"I understand. I think." My whole body sank, jealous of his attachment to his dead wife.

"Listen. I've got to take some time off."

"Of course. You've been working nonstop on Lee's painting."

"From our relationship."

I told myself not to crumble but I was melting into a dark hole. "What are you saying?"

"I don't know what I'm saying. I care for you. We've had some incredible times. I need to see my children and focus on my work here. I'm sorry. I can't explain it."

"I'm a big girl," I said stiffly. "But if there is someone else, David, just tell me. Please don't drag this out." I was about to burst into tears but didn't want him to sense my utter devastation.

"No, no. There's no one else. Well, no one except the ghost of my deceased wife."

Those words were a thousand knives going through me. To compete with a living woman was one thing, but to compete with the memory of a woman was more than I could take. A woman who was prettier, smarter, thinner, sexier. It was a no-win situation.

"I feel like Marsha Mason in Neil Simon's movie

Second Chance but without her fighting spirit."

"Please give me some time."

"How much time are you talking about?"

"I don't know. A few months."

"David. I've got to go." I had to hang up. Otherwise he would have heard me cry uncontrollably. My heart was tumbling over a cliff down further and further. How could he do this? After all we'd been through? We could have been killed. We discovered a treasure trove. Weren't we meant to be together? I felt drawn and quartered. My heart pulled in one way, my mind another way, my body another way. Wild horses ripping me apart.

30

Washington, D.C.

I watched dozens of movies the following week. One after the other. But nothing with Kevin Klein or Clint Eastwood in them. Nothing that would remind me of David. *Harold and Maude* was one of my all time favorites and it was so much better watching it in its high-definition format. Ruth Gordon was a great actress and role model, working into her eighties. *Auntie Mame* with Rosalind Russell was another classic. 'Live, live, live' was their message. "Get hurt even," Maude told Harold in the movie. I knew how to do that.

Phillip had called a couple of times but I had been too depressed to call him back. One night I forgot to check the caller ID and ended up making a dinner date with him.

"You've been a hard woman to reach," Phillip said as I locked my front door and we walked down my brick steps.

"It's been a busy fall," I said with a fake smile.

Phillip had never picked me up for dinner before. He took my arm gently and led me to the open door of the limousine. A uniformed driver with hat nodded at me.

"Where are we going, Phillip?"

"You'll see."

We drove past the White House and stopped in front of the Willard Hotel.

"Have you been to the Occidental before?"

"Not for a long time." Bill Trevor had taken me to the Occidental Restaurant twenty years ago. I had been so nervous I ordered chopped sirloin because it was the least expensive item on the menu, not realizing it was glorified hamburger meat. Bill had ordered the most expensive entree and later told his mother how the dinner had put a big dent in his pocket. What a child I was then.

"We'll take a bottle of Dom Pèrignon," Phillip told the waiter.

"Did you sell a shipload of books?" I looked at Phillip in wonderment.

"Thought we'd celebrate your safe return from your European travels. And after you blew me off, I figured I better assert myself."

Phillip was a different person, or at least more the person I had imagined him to be when we first met. Distance made the heart grow fonder, indeed. We had a lively chat about his latest appearances. He actually asked me questions about my work and about the art discovered in Germany. I was glad to have the distraction. I had cried my eyes out over David. It had been a week and a half since his devastating phone call but I still was on eggshells.

"To think you were actually ensnarled by a notorious art criminal. You could write a bestseller about it," Phillip smiled in a way I had never seen.

"It certainly is an experience I don't want to repeat."

The champagne was making me feel better. I ordered the most exotic gourmet entrée the restaurant offered. Phillip ordered a great 2007 Cabernet. After the waiter had cleared our dinner plates, Phillip looked at me intently. "I have a surprise for you." He reached into his pocket and placed a small, fancy black box in front of me. I stared at it. Maybe it wasn't what I thought.

"Go on. Open it," he said playfully.

The stiff hinge gave way to a stunning diamond ring. "Phillip.... I don't know what to say."

"Put it on. I know we haven't talked about our relationship much, but I wanted you to know I'm serious. And although I don't show my emotions well, I am very fond of you."

I would have been thrilled with this scene two months ago.

"Phillip, I'm not ready for this. I'm...." I could not bring myself to mention David.

"Don't be ridiculous. It's only a ring." Phillip picked up the tiny black box, removed the three-carat ring, and slipped it on my finger.

"See how it feels," he said.

It was dazzling. I had always wanted an emerald cut diamond. But I couldn't be intimate with him right now. How could I fend him off after dinner? My emotions were raw. Was David the real thing? Or Phillip? I had no idea.

"Now that I have your attention, let's talk about when you're coming to Dallas."

At that moment a handsome man in a dark suit and purple tie approached our table.

"Phillip, what are you doing in Washington?" he asked.

Phillip was out of his chair. "Ashton, hi. I could ask you the same. Millicent, this is Ashton James. My publisher with Random House. Ashton, Millicent Clermont from the National Gallery."

Good, he didn't introduce me as his fiancé. I shook Ashton's hand. He looked more like an investment banker than a publisher.

"Join us, Ashton. What are you drinking?"

"Oh, I don't want to interrupt your dinner," Ashton said as his hands went up.

"No interruption at all. We're finished. Please sit down," Phillip said as he pulled out a chair for Ashton.

We talked about the future of publishing, e-books, and the catastrophic changes in print media, including the demise of bookstores.

"There is nothing better than sitting down with a

hardcover book," I interjected. "To look closely at the texture of the paper, the font, to roll my eyes over the letters, individual characters forming a word, jewels in a setting." I glanced at the shining ring on my finger, then smiled weakly at Phillip.

"Wow, where did you find her, Phillip? I wish more people shared your sensibilities, Millicent," Ashton said with raised eyebrows.

Out of the corner of my eye, I could see Phillip beaming at me. And then in a nanosecond his attention shifted.

"Are you staying at the Willard?" Phillip asked Ashton.

"I am. I'm catching the shuttle back to New York in the morning."

"Can you fit in a thirty-minute meeting? I wanted to give you my ideas on my next novel." Phillip leaned toward Ashton.

"Phillip, why don't I take a cab home so you and Ashton can keep talking? I've got an early morning breakfast with a donor." It wasn't true but this was going to save me. From his expression, it was obvious he was glad I offered.

"Sure you don't mind, Millicent?" Phillip pored on the charm.

"No, really I don't." I looked at Ashton. "It was nice meeting you."

"I'll walk you out." Phillip led me out the door.

"Thank you for being so understanding. You're an angel." He waved his rented limo over and opened the door for me.

"It was quite an evening, Phillip. I…"

"Don't say another word. I'll call you tomorrow." He kissed me quickly and helped me into the back seat. I admired the glittering ring on my finger in the dark car as it reflected the lights going home alone via limousine.

I let myself in to my empty townhouse, went to the kitchen to get ice water and returned to the living room. I turned on my DVD player and inserted *Incognito*, a film I had ordered through Netflix. I got teased at work about still using the U.S. mail and not downloading my DVDs. But just as I loved hardback and paperback books rather than reading on a Kindle, I liked my rented films delivered to my mailbox.

I settled into the sofa and punched 'play.' Gorgeous Jason Patric played Harry Donovan, a talented artist who painted forgeries for a living. When shady art dealers approached Harry to create a fake Rembrandt, Harry agreed to do it. While Harry was in Paris researching Rembrandt, he met a Rembrandt scholar, played by French actress Irène Jacob, who later was called in to authenticate Harry's fake Rembrandt. Despite their romantic entanglement, she confirmed the talent of the artist but wouldn't authenticate it as a true Rembrandt.

The art dealers later double-crossed Harry, framing him for murder and theft of 'their Rembrandt.' At his trial, Harry proceeded to paint another fake Rembrandt to prove his innocence, obviously inspired by Han van Meegeren's real life story. But Harry put down his brush, knowing he would be wrongly convicted, because he could no longer paint forgeries.

I loved this movie! The making of forgeries, authentications, the greed of art dealers, the struggle of artists, real versus fake. Why hadn't I heard of *Incognito*? Terrible films such as *Terminator* made millions of dollars, while this beautifully executed film received only modest success despite its excellent actors dialogue, plot, and cinematography. It made no sense. It was disgusting: commercial versus artful.

The next morning Andrew's distinctive drawl on the other end of my phone woke me up. "Millicent, have you seen the papers?"

"Good morning, Andrew. No, I'm still in bed."

"Call me back once you see it. I want to know what you think of the article I wrote."

"Okay. Let me drink a cup of coffee. What page is it on?" I yawned.

"You can't miss it, dah-ling. It's on the front page."

I slipped on my robe, ran downstairs, and grabbed the paper from my steps. Thank heavens *The Washington Post* was still a real paper. I spread it open and saw in big headlines:

GALLERY EXEC FINDS TREASURES IN CHURCH

Andrew had written a terrific article that included all the details of our trip to Wiesen. Separate photos of Haywood, David, and me were on the inside. I stared at the picture of David.

They even ran photos of Otto and Max Baader. Max was only slightly more disheveled in his mug shot than he looked when he pretended to be Theodore Pennington. What a lot of ink for the Gallery. Andrew's article went on to say that National Gallery curators were headed to Paris to identify the discovered art housed at the Louvre. The article was very complimentary of me. It sounded as if I would be the happiest person in the world.

I picked up my phone and called Andrew. "It's absolutely fabulous. Thank you for the great coverage," I told him.

"One never knows what the editor is going to do with a story. But I was quite pleased."

"I'll have to buy a bunch of copies. My fifteen minutes of fame. Thanks again, Andrew."

"You're famous, dah-ling."

Where was the accompanying happiness? I felt empty. I wondered if I would send David a copy.

I decided to call Diane, the psychic.

I told her about David. "We were so incredibly close and then he pulled away," my voice broke.

"He's not the only one tied to the past," Diane said.

"What are you saying?"

"That young man who died when you were in college. You haven't let go of him."

"Of course. I loved Bill. He and his mother mean so much to me."

"Yes, I understand that. But he's become your ghostly lover," Diane said.

"Ghostly lover?"

"Esther Harding wrote about it in her book, *Way of All Women*. It's when a woman remains attached to a former lover and it prevents her from forming a new relationship."

"We weren't even lovers, technically. We were downright chaste compared to today's standards."

"It has little or nothing to do with whether you consummated your relationship. You measure men against your idealization of him, so no man can really make the grade. He's always in the background, like a ghost."

"But that's not how I think of David. I love David. I want to be with him."

"Yes, but you must let go of your past and then David can let go of his. That is the way the universe works. You must become completely empty so that a new relationship can take root. Think of it as clearing out your garden. Trying to plant on top of existing material will get you in trouble."

"So you think David and I will get back together?"

"Millicent, I use astrology to access my psychic gift but you and David both have free will. I can see patterns and can help you analyze what is going on in your life. But what you do is up to you and the choices you make. Astrology can be useful as an analytical tool to know the self. That's why Carl Jung studied astrology.

"Astrology can be used for good or for evil," Diane continued. "Hitler, before he came to power, regularly consulted an astrologer who was also a hypnotist. Erik Jan Hanussen taught Hitler mass psychology, dramatic speaking, and crowd control. Hitler's inner circle also used astrology. Hess' astrologer Karl Krafft made several accurate predictions that didn't sit well with Hitler and for that he was imprisoned and died in a concentration camp. I didn't mean to give you a short history on Nazism and astrology. But you are seeking an understanding of World War II as it relates to Nazi-looted art."

"That's for sure." I walked over to my coffee maker, poured myself another cup, and put a generous amount of milk in it. I switched the phone to my other ear.

"Back to your current lesson," Diane said. "You need to clear out negative energy from your mind and heart. Let go of anything that gets in the way of your goals and purpose. We can cherish our memories of loved ones who are on another plane, but we cannot let their memories create negative energy. Every soul has its own individual path. Bill changed your life. Your father changed your life. Now both of them are working out the next stages of their own soul paths in a fantastic world we know little about. Whatever our losses are—whether it's a lover, a pet, or something material—they teach us something about ourselves and can move us closer to God."

We ended the call. She would send me a CD of the session; I would send her a check.

Once again I became highly irritated after listening to Diane. My initial response was *no, that's not right.* Then after I processed what she said, my resistance broke down. But how did one love and then let go?

Still in my robe, I climbed the stairs to my bedroom and pulled out Bill's letters from my dresser. They were still intact despite their twenty years. I carefully removed the satin ribbon, unfolded each one and then read them in the order he had written them. In one he wrote: "You think the weekends are endless, but they're not. Talk your peeps into letting you come down to C'ville." In another one, Bill quoted from a current song: "….child of Springtime, still green, lying there by the road…" How prophetic could these letters have been? He died on the side of the road after his friend's Porsche crashed. I read and reread the poem he wrote for me. The last four lines were my favorite.

"But still I often wonder could she have been real
Or is she the reason why I sometimes feel
That beauty is not something seen with eyes
But a reflection of a longing deep inside."

I gathered Bill's letters and took them downstairs. I fetched matches from the kitchen and sat in front of my fireplace. I lit the letters one by one and tossed them into the hearth. Each one ignited in a red and yellow flickering flame, then died to black ashes. Letter after letter. Flame to black. Forever gone. I stared at the black fireplace, then went upstairs and took a shower until the water ran cold.

31

Dallas

Flying in a private plane to Love Field was not a bad way to travel. Phillip picked me up in a silver Jaguar, stepping out of his car in his signature leather jacket and cowboy boots. Why was I here? The real reason was to break it off with Phillip face to face.

"Welcome to Texas," Phillip said.

"Remember I'm a Texan too."

It took us a mere fifteen minutes to reach Phillip's high-rise condo on Turtle Creek. It was contemporary, filled with expensive furniture. Lots of books. Light on the art.

"Fantastic view of downtown Dallas," I marveled at the vista.

"And no one can ever block the view," Phillip boasted.

"What is this painting?" I peered at a café scene.

"Actually that's a giclée. The Museum of Modern Art has them. It's the highest quality computer-generated reproduction you can buy."

"Yes, I'm familiar with giclées. The applied paint strokes give it the appearance of a real painting."

"Hurry and get dressed, Millicent. We're having dinner at Zaza's, a really fun place."

I slipped into a slinky teal dress and matching high heels. This was what I had wanted from the first night I had met Phillip. But now I was in love with David. And David might never call me back. He may never leave his past.

"You look mah-vo-lous," Phillip said mimicking Billy Crystal. "Let's go. I want to take you shopping before dinner."

"The Crescent Court is owned by Caroline Hunt of the famous Hunt family," Phillip said as we drove to the front of Stanley Korshak. "You know, the old man had three families all going at once."

"Yes, Caroline and her sister Margaret went to my alma mater, Mary Baldwin College."

"I hope they're more generous than their father. He was rich as God but didn't support local charities and businesses, something Dallas establishment didn't appreciate."

"Margaret, when she was living, and Caroline to this day have done tremendous things for Mary Baldwin, including renovating Hill Top, the inspiration for my doll house."

"Oh, yeah. That."

We entered the high-end boutique walking past

luscious scented candles. Phillip took me straight to the jewelry counter. "I've picked out some bracelets for you."

Acknowledging Phillip, the stylish sales woman took two gorgeous wide cuffs out of the case, black enamel with pearls. "Very Coco Chanel."

Phillip snapped them on my wrists. They were beautiful.

"You look perfect now." Phillip pulled out his credit card.

"Thank you, Phillip," I said, not knowing what else to do in the situation.

Zaza's was across the street from Stanley Korstak but in Dallas across the street was still a car ride. When Phillip escorted me into the restaurant, I couldn't help but think of him as a peacock in erect fantail. Zaza's décor was fun and the food delicious. Phillip kept scanning the dinner crowd. It was obvious he was disappointed he didn't see someone he knew, or more importantly, someone who knew him. I was nothing more than his accessory. Everything was perfect on the outside. Nothing on the inside had any meaning whatsoever.

When we got back to his condo, Phillip loosened his tie and unbuttoned his shirt. He started unzipping my dress. I moved away.

"Phillip, that was a lovely dinner. Thank you for bringing me to Dallas. But we need to talk about our relationship."

"Fine." Phillip sat down and turned on the television and focused on the screen.

"No, we need to talk. Without any interference."

"I can hardly wait." He turned off the television with an angry click.

I took the ring off my finger and placed it gently on the coffee table. "This is a beautiful ring. Some woman is going to love it. I thought this was what I wanted. Thank you for the fun ride. And promise me I won't show up in one of your novels."

He gave a weak smile.

I took off the bracelets and placed them next to the ring.

"Keep the bracelets."

"Thank you, but no. In my heart of hearts, I know this is the right thing. And I think you know it too."

I stood up and went into the bedroom. Sad but relieved. I changed into my nightgown and lay down. I heard Phillip getting a drink, turning on the television, flipping channels, and then I was out.

In the morning, the silence in the apartment hung in the air like death. Phillip put a K-cup in the coffeemaker. I waited until his coffee was made and he removed his cup. I then made one for myself.

"Phillip…"

"Don't say anything."

I finally broke the stifling silence. "Can't we both just

recognize that we were attracted to each other but in the final analysis we realized it wasn't going to work? Does that mean we have to be enemies?"

His lack of response spoke volumes.

I slept all the way to Reagan National. I knew I had taken the right course in ending it with Phillip. I was learning the utter emptiness of mere materialism. The old me would have kept the cuff bracelets he had given me.

As much as I loved beauty in all its forms—fine art, architecture, jewelry, clothes, homes, furnishings—I realized owning them could not add one iota of value to my soul.

I appreciated and admired the artistry and work that went into creating any beautiful work of art, but it dawned on me that I had desperately needed my luxury tags and wanted these material markers to fill a void within me.

It wasn't that I would throw out what I had. The radical difference was my attachment to these things. Was David the reason I had changed?

Did I have to trade this spiritual truth for loneliness?

I opened the door to my deadly quiet townhouse. Now I had no men in my life. Feast or famine. Periods of famine were not new to me. How long would this one last? There were advantages to living alone. No one to belittle me. No disagreements over buying furniture or clothes. No one to clean up after. No one.

32

Washington, D.C.

I turned out the light in my bedroom, emotionally exhausted. Soon we would find out whether Lee's painting was a Vermeer. Soon Lee would find out if the I.R.S. would give her a tax credit. Someday the lawsuit would be a thing of the past. At least I didn't have to have F.B.I. coverage anymore. As nice as the guys were, I was glad to have my privacy back.

Please God, please let Lee's painting be a Vermeer. And please bring David back to me. Amen.

I dreamed someone was holding my mouth and I couldn't breathe. When I opened my eyes, I tried to scream but nothing came out. Even in my darkened bedroom, I could see a young man with a shaven head on top of me. His rough hand over my lips. Then I caught sight of the knife blade close to my jaw.

"Don't make a fucking sound or I'll cut your throat," he said.

I shook my head slightly. I tried to tell him I couldn't breathe. He moved his hand slightly which reeked of tobacco. As my sight adjusted to the dark, I noticed a tattoo on his neck. It showed a Celtic cross with the words 'White Pride World Wide' around it.

"You bitch, do you know what you've done? You've ruined my life," he ranted at me.

I mumbled through the human muzzle. Tears streamed from my eyes.

"Stop crying. I'm going to take my hand off your mouth but if you so much as whimper, blood will be gushing out of you so fast you'll get to see yourself die."

I slowly shook my head. "How…"

He slapped me hard across the face. "I told you not to say one fucking word."

My face crumpled up in pain and fear, tears flowing, nose running, cheek stinging.

"When you and your nigger F.B.I. boy got to messing around, you put my father and uncle in jail. And I was depending on that stupid art to fund my activities. Now because of you, you two-bit whore, Hammerskin Nation will have to cancel our concert in D.C."

The sins of the father visited upon the sons and grandsons. Nazi, neo-Nazi. Who was going to rescue me this time? *Please God, help me.* Was this how I was going to die? As if in answer to my prayer, the intruder got off me and stood next to the bed but kept the knife close to my throat. I took a deep breath. He wore a t-shirt with suspenders and combat boots. I saw a flight jacket on the floor.

"Now, here's what you are going to do to stay alive. You are going to give me ten million dollars. You were married to a rich kid. He can give it to you. I want you to tell him to put it in a backpack marked with a Celtic cross on a park bench in Lafayette Square. If he doesn't, I'll kill you. If you contact your nigger boy, I'll kill you. Call your ex right now. And if you make one false move, I'll rape you and then I'll kill you."

My whole body ached with dry fear. How did he know who my ex-husband was? I motioned to the phone. He handed it to me. Who should I call? I couldn't call my ex-husband Turny. I had no idea where he was or how he would respond. David? Phillip? I needed to figure out who would be reachable. I dialed Andrew's number.

"Millicent, top of the morning to you," Andrew began.

"Before you say another word, Turny," I cut him off. "I need your help. I need ten million dollars. Immediately. I can't explain. Go to Lafayette Square and put the money in a backpack marked with a Celtic cross on the park bench facing the White House. The deadline is eight a.m. Then I will be released. That's all I can say."

Andrew whistled softly.

"Thank you, Turny," I said in a mechanical way, and hung up before Andrew could blow my ruse.

Daylight began filling the room. I looked at the

clock. Six thirty. How long had this neo-Nazi thug been in my home?

"I've got to go the bathroom," I said, wondering if my captor would let me.

"I'll go with you. Don't try any shit."

Pun intended. I got out of bed and walked toward my bathroom with the skinhead following me, his knife drawn. I sat on the toilet while he watched me. I flushed and indicated I wanted to wash my hands. My splotchy face in the mirror showed the welt from his slap and my swollen eyes. He pointed with his knife motioning me back to the bedroom. I got in bed and pulled the covers up around me.

He began looking around my bedroom. "You moved that chair and table," he said.

A cold chill washed over me. "You were the one who broke in last month. I don't think your mother would approve of you breaking into people's homes."

"Shut the fuck up. My mother's dead." He looked out the window.

"What's your tattoo mean?" I asked tentatively.

"You been hiding under a rock? It stands for Stormfront. There's 150,000 of us and we're going to get rid of the niggers and spics, and fags and Jews." He pointed his finger at me. "We're going to get this piece of crap country to back to where it used to be."

"Are you a skinhead?"

"Do I look like a skinhead?"

"Yes, you do."

"Well, that makes me a skinhead."

Then I noticed a tattoo on his arm. It said Leo. "Is your name Leo?"

"Aren't you're smart? But if you don't shut up, I'll make sure you can't talk."

Surely Andrew had called the F.B.I. by now. Why didn't they know about him? I wished I could call my mother. I promised to be a better daughter if I lived through this.

My captor paced as the minutes ticked by. Looking out the windows. Checking his watch. Glaring at me. He checked his watch for the hundredth time. "Okay, let's go."

"Go? Go where?" My stomach felt hungry and sick at the same time.

"To get the money, stupid."

"I need to get dressed. I mean, if I went outside in my nightgown, people will stare."

"Hurry up. Remember killing you will earn me red shoelaces."

I went into my closet, pulled jeans on, a turtleneck and sweater.

"Where's your car?"

"It's parked down the street."

"We're going to walk to it and you are going to act normal or I'll cut your face up so bad your mother won't want to see you."

He put on his jacket and grabbed my arm. As we went down the stairs, I could feel the knife tip in my back. He squeezed my arm tighter as he closed the door behind us.

The street was virtually empty on this Saturday morning. No sign of any police officers. We got into my Volvo, which was parked down the street. Why weren't my neighbors out walking their dogs or something?

"Drive to Lafayette Square."

Still no sign of police or F.B.I. as I drove slowly to the park. Leo ordered me out of the car. He had me firmly in his grip. He motioned me toward the park bench. Hadn't Andrew called someone to rescue me? Where were they?

At least a backpack sat on the designated bench. A homeless person wearing a battered hat and dirty mismatched clothes shuffled toward the bench. My captor picked up his pace, pushing me ahead of him. The rumpled man stopped in front of the backpack and reached for the canvas bag.

"Hey, bum! Get your hands off of that. It's mine." Leo rushed to the man, squeezing my arm harder as he pulled me along. The unshaven man turned slowly. Then his hands became a magician's, clamping handcuffs on Leo's wrists and pulling him to the ground. I recognized him as one of the agents who used to guard my house.

"You waited long enough," I said, stepping back with a deep sigh.

"Sorry, Millicent. We didn't want to take a chance."

Leo the Neo cussed up a storm as Haywood and two other agents ran up.

"You all right, Millicent?" I heard Haywood's voice as I collapsed.

Haywood drove my car back to my townhouse. I was still shaking.

"You shouldn't stay at your house," Haywood said.

"I'm not going back there." I ran through various options. I didn't want to get on a plane. I just needed a place to crash. Someplace I wasn't alone. "Haywood, I think I'll go to the Four Seasons. It's close. Would you go inside with me so I can get my clothes? I'm afraid all my bravery juice is gone."

"You've been through quite an ordeal. A five-star hotel will do you some good."

Haywood parked in front of my townhouse putting an F.B.I. ID on the dashboard. He walked upstairs with me. When I saw my bed, I shuddered. The knife at my throat, the disgusting skinhead on top of me. My knees buckled and I broke into a body-torqueing sob on the floor.

Haywood lifted me up and set me in my slipper chair.

"Millicent, you're safe now. No one can hurt you."

I regained my composure but had to get out of my house as soon as possible. I threw some makeup and clothes in a small suitcase. I added a pocket prayer book.

In a matter of minutes we were walking up to the front desk of the Four Seasons. I left my sunglasses on to hide my eyes.

"Are you sure you'll be okay alone?" Haywood asked as he put his hand on my shoulder.

"Could you make sure there aren't any other Baader family members lined up to kill me?"

"I promise you there's no one else. But when you get ready to return home, give me a call. We'll get coverage on your place again until you feel safe." Haywood turned and left.

I gave the pretty hotel receptionist my credit card, took my key card, and followed the bellman to the elevators. He opened the door to a luxurious suite, put my bag on a luggage rack, and left with a generous tip. I plopped on the queen size bed, ordered room service, and fell dead asleep.

The knock at the door startled me. At first I didn't remember where I was. A waiter rolled in the room service table. I poured a glass of wine and took the prayer book out of my suitcase. After my equilibrium was restored, I called Andrew.

"Millicent, I am so relieved to hear your voice," Andrew said. "Where are you?"

"I'm sorry I didn't call you before…I'm at the Four Seasons, but thank you for saving my life."

"The F.B.I. did that, dah-ling. I only made the call."

"I'd invite you up for a drink, but I'm not too sure how long I'm going to last."

"You should rest. We'll celebrate later."

The next morning I got a massage and then went shopping on M Street. My cell phone rang. "Hi, Haywood…. I'm much better. I'm walking down M Street right this second…Okay, see you there in five minutes."

I opened the brass and glass door of Clyde's, a restaurant I had been going to for years. Haywood was seated in the old bar section. I slid into the booth and we both ordered burgers.

"Richard Green's assistant was being paid by the lawyer who sued us?" I took a big drink of my red wine in anger.

"The New York lawyer was paying her a thousand dollars a month to email him pictures of the artwork coming into the gallery. When Lee's painting came through, he found it on the list of Nazi looted art and who claimed it."

"And filed a lawsuit before any attempt at negotiation."

"Bigger fee that way," Haywood deduced.

"Thank God Colette and Jacques are nice people and not controlled by their lawyer."

"The lawyer also paid the writer who wrote the story in the online magazine. Too bad Rupert Murdoch closed down *News of the World.* They both could have worked there." Haywood took a bite out of his hamburger.

"By the way, how is Richard Green?" I asked.

"He's out of the hospital. He's happy to have lost weight but doesn't recommend ingesting arsenic to do it. Of course he fired his assistant, but she'll show up at another gallery in town." Haywood shook his head.

We finished our lunch and got up to leave.

"How long are you planning to stay at the Four Seasons?"

"You know, I could get used to that kind of service."

"I bet you could," Haywood said as he opened the door for me.

Once back at the hotel, I called Andrew.

"Oh, Mill-i-cent." He had never sounded that way.

"Andrew, want to come to the Four Seasons for dinner? It's the least I can do for saving my life."

"I'm not in the best of spirits. Well, I am in the spirits. Something dreadful has occurred."

"What, Andrew?"

"I shall not be able to hide it forever. You might as well know now. Can you come here? I can't be seen in public right now."

"I'll be right there, Andrew."

I hurried along the cobblestone streets to Andrew's townhouse. I looked at my townhouse next door and shuddered. I knocked on his door.

"Millicent, please excuse my appearance." Andrew ushered me in. Instead of a highly starched look, Andrew's wrinkled shirt was hanging outside his trousers. A look I had never seen on him.

"Come in. The place is a mess. I told Pearl not to come today."

"Looks fine to me." I could not detect anything that had changed in his over the top townhouse.

Andrew brushed his forehead. "Where are my manners? May I get you a cocktail?"

"No, thank you. I'm fine."

We sat down in our regular places. Andrew in his cracked leather wing chair, I sank into the matching chair opposite the game table.

"Andrew, I've never seen you like this."

He took out a cigarette and lit it. "This morning I received a phone call from the curatorial committee identifying the art you discovered in Germany," he said in a dull voice. "Apparently I am heir to one of the stolen paintings. A painting worth seven hundred thousand dollars."

"Andrew, that's fantastic!"

"The painting belonged to the Rothschilds from whom it was stolen during the war."

"What am I missing here?"

"Millicent, the Rothschilds were Jewish and apparently I am a direct descendant. I am a member of many clubs in which one's pedigree is important. If I claim the painting, and God knows I could use the resources, I don't know how I will be treated."

"Because you have a tiny bit of Jewish blood?" People's views never ceased to astound me.

Andrew nodded.

"So you never knew?"

"Our family has prided itself on its Anglo ancestry for three hundred years."

I left Andrew's and wandered back to the Four Seasons. What a bizarre turn of events. Lee's painting had set off all sorts of cosmic events. My cell phone chimed.

"Millie?"

"Hi, Mommy."

"I have some bad news. Godiva had a heart attack swimming in the lake."

"How is she?"

"She's in dog heaven."

I burst into tears.

"She had a good life, Millie."

"Don't say that," I said, repeating my best friend's admonition.

"She died doing her favorite thing. I hope I die that way." My mother's attempts at consoling me were useless. I searched my purse for more Kleenex.

"Where is Godiva now?"

"The vet came and got her. I could have her cremated and send you the ashes. You could take them to that cemetery in Paris."

"Père-Lachaise. The name of the cemetery is Père-Lachaise. Thanks for calling, Mommy. I'll call you later. I love you."

I dabbed my eyes as I approached the entrance to the hotel. I was sure my mascara was horribly smeared. I started thinking about taking Godiva's ashes to Paris and burst into tears again. I quickly walked to the elevator with my head down.

Once in my suite, I fell on the bed and emptied the rest of my tears on the pillow.

Later I reapplied my makeup and went back out for a long walk around Georgetown. I avoided the corner where Godiva had made her impression in wet cement. I headed up Wisconsin and then turned around. I didn't need to relive a David memory by walking past Bistro Lepic.

I didn't want to go home, but I couldn't afford to stay at the Four Seasons any longer. There wasn't any place I could think of that didn't bring back bad memories of the last few weeks. There were so many things beyond my control. Hadn't I learned enough lessons? Wasn't it time for some good news?

33

National Gallery of Art
Whittington Plantation

I picked up my ringing office phone.

Amy, the director's assistant, was on the other end. "The director wants to see you as soon as possible. He and Paul Morton have something to tell you."

"Oh my gosh. I'll be right there." My knees literally were shaking. This was the defining hour. Would Lee be able to hold onto Whittington? If her painting is a real Vermeer, we're home free. If they have decided it is not a real Vermeer, Lee will lose Whittington and the Alexanders will accelerate their lawsuit. *Please God, let this come out the right way. I'll do anything. Even give up David.*

My heart became a drum at a tribal dance. I looked at each step of the white staircase, how it darkened where the risers met each carpeted tread. I tried to read Amy's body language as I passed her before reaching the director's office threshold. She was focused on her computer screen. No information there. I saw John and Paul going over a list, heads down.

"John? Paul?" I was near tears.

"Come in, Millicent," John said giving me no clue. "Have a seat."

This didn't look good. I sat next to Paul in the empty chair across from John's desk.

"Paul, tell her."

"Millicent," he said slowly, "we have spent an inordinate amount of time on the Whittington painting."

Yes, I know that. Just bloody tell me.

"And after careful analysis," Paul dragged on, "we have concluded that the painting is indeed an original work of art by Jan Vermeer."

"It is? It is?" I stood up. "You're saying it is a real Vermeer?"

"It is."

"Paul, thank you!" I grabbed both his hands and shook them.

"John, thank you!" I grabbed his hands but then pulled back. "I can't thank you enough. You don't know what this means to Lee Trevor. Now if you'll excuse me, I've got to call her." I turned to go.

"Wait." John's hand was up.

"Is there a catch?" I asked.

"There are two matters that need to be addressed," John said. "One, you need to get Mrs. Trevor to agree to convey half the painting to the Gallery. And two, you need to help raise fifty million dollars to pay the Alexanders for the other half."

"Is that all?" I screamed as ran out of the office to call Lee with the good news.

Coming into the lane, I rolled down the car windows and listened. The crunch of gravel followed us through the canopied trees, the open fields, past the magnolias and the "Slow Peacocks" sign. No matter how many times I had driven down this lane, the white mansion was hidden and then appeared out of nowhere, big, dramatic, iconic. The gingko tree had dropped its golden leaves creating a glorious yellow carpet.

Haywood and I walked up the steps, the boxwood wrapping me in its scent. Lee had left the door open so I spoke through the screen door. "Lee? We're here."

Lee came through her sitting room door. "Yes, come in Millicent. Haywood, please come in." Lee ushered us out to the sun porch.

"We've only a few days left before it will be too cold to be out here, so I thought we should take advantage of it," Lee said. "May I offer you a glass of wine?" She gestured toward a bottle in a silver cooler covered in condensation.

"That sounds great, Lee," I said.

"As you can imagine, I've been anxious for your arrival." Lee looked at both of us.

I poured wine for the three of us. "Isn't it exciting that your painting is a real Vermeer?"

"To think all those years we never knew. And, Haywood," Lee said as she turned to him, "I have you to thank. You know I was shocked when you told me my painting had been stolen. And I'm afraid I was rude."

"I understand. No problem," Haywood said. "I am sorry for the trauma I caused you. But a happy ending is close at hand."

"Oh?" Lee's eyebrows shot up.

"Now the true provenance of your painting is known," Haywood said, "the next step is to work out a suitable agreement between you and the Alexander heirs. One possible scenario is that you convey half the value of the painting to the National Gallery. The National Gallery would pay the Alexanders for the other half of the painting. And *Lady in Waiting* would be on display for the public to enjoy at the National Gallery and at the Louvre. Once an agreement is reached, Millicent can start raising the money from private donors to pay the Alexanders."

"Has this sort of arrangement been done before?" Lee asked.

"The Art Institute in Chicago negotiated these same terms over Degas' *Landscape with Smokestacks*," Haywood replied.

"The problem is that the tax deduction I would receive won't do me much good," Lee said as she looked out the tall windows to the expansive fields.

"I called on the general counsel at the I.R.S.," I

interjected. "Mr. Milbank is considering a tax credit since in essence you are donating the painting to the federal government."

"That truly would be an answer to prayer," Lee said.

"It would." I exhaled.

"I hope you don't mind," Haywood said, "but I took the liberty of paying a visit to Johnson Milbank myself on your behalf, Lee. And if you are agreeable to conveying your painting to the National Gallery, the I.R.S. will allow you a tax credit for half the value of the painting, which would be fifty million dollars."

"I can't believe you, Haywood. That is wonderful!" I beamed at him and at Lee.

"That is the best news of all," Lee said and smiled for the first time. "Of course I will convey *Lady in Waiting* to the National Gallery."

She looked again through the windows to the limitless landscape. "We think we live in our separate worlds safe from the evils of the past until one day we are confronted with its reality. That is what happened on your first visit, Haywood. I could not ignore the horror of the Holocaust or the horror of slavery. Then shortly afterward, my husband's business dealings long after he died threatened everything I have. And now you, Haywood, of all people, whose ancestors lived here, have made it possible for me to keep Whittington. Thank you."

"I'm glad I could help," Haywood said.

The sun illuminated the boxwood, trees, and fields

outside the casement windows, warming the sun porch with rays of light, happy as a Thomas Cole painting.

"Lee, I hate to leave so soon, but I've got to get back to D.C.," I said.

"Oh, I hate that you have to leave too."

We stood and walked toward the front door. I hugged Lee. "I'll call you soon."

Haywood held out his hand to shake Lee's. Instead Lee hugged him. "You are a remarkable person, Haywood. Thank you again," Lee said.

With that miracle, we left.

34

National Gallery of Art
Washington, D.C.

The Rotunda in the West Building, its center dome reaching toward the heavens and its voluminous flowers encircling the signature bronze statue of Apollo, was electric with excitement. Black-clad waiters buzzed around tables festooned with silk cloths and artful floral arrangements, place cards carefully positioned. The guest list had been meticulously checked.

Former Justice Sandra Day O'Conner was coming, as she did frequently to Gallery events. Directors from major museums around the country were attending: the Metropolitan, the Art Institute, the Gardner. Even representatives from the Louvre and Musée d'Orsay, the Prado and Thyssen-Bornemisza were coming. As I scanned the guest list, I stopped cold. I couldn't believe what I saw. Petrides Wilde was on the list. How could he? His two brothers and nephew were in custody for trying to kill me. This man had no conscience.

I checked my watch. Guests would be arriving in ten minutes. I went to the ladies room.

My make-up was fine. My new purple silk Nicole Miller was flattering. Okay, it looked really good on me. Everything on the outside was fine. I was thrilled that everyone I cared about would be here to share this evening of celebration. Everyone, except David. Everything was perfect except the crater in my heart. That and the beautiful devil Pet Wilde coming. Maybe he wouldn't show.

I returned to the Rotunda. My mother was the first to arrive.

"Mimi, hi!" I waved her over. She had done it again. She had put herself together like a phoenix rising out of the ashes looking gorgeous in her off-white and gold outfit. She had flown to D.C. two days ago and had already created her signature Kandinsky chaos in my guest bedroom.

"There's Haywood. I can't wait to introduce you." I guided my proud mother over to meet him.

"Ah, the woman of the hour," Haywood exuded as I approached.

I smiled meekly and shook my head. "Haywood, this is my mother Catherine Clermont."

"You have one brave and terrific daughter, Mrs. Clermont," Haywood pronounced.

"She is," my mother said. "And to think we would have never known if she had not heard your lecture in

October."

"Feel free to continue your adoration of me. I'll be right back. I told Lee I'd meet her at the entrance. Our table is at the front. See you there in a sec."

Lee Trevor, wearing her signature sapphire color, was walking in as I approached the door. We maneuvered our way to the Rotunda among the arriving guests who rewarded fashion houses' latest designs. I was overwhelmed that we were going to the head table past many of my donors and colleagues. Lee and my mother greeted each other. They had met several years ago when I had taken Mimi to Whittington. Lee warmly said hello to Haywood. Then Colette and Jacques made their grand entrance, looking every bit the French aristocrats that they were.

Colette kissed me on both cheeks. "Bonsoir, mon amie." Her jewelry was magnificent. A necklace of large black pearls and diamonds against her translucent skin set off the black ruffles at her neck.

Jacques kissed my hand. His navy velvet jacket and ascot were stunning. I introduced them around the table.

Following the Alexanders, Gabby arrived. As usual she had stepped out of the pages of *Town & Country* with her navy silk pantsuit and Jimmy Choo shoes, the most understated and sophisticated one in the room.

"Gabby, I am so thrilled you're here!" We hugged and per her custom she handed me a gift, this time a small box from Tiffany's.

"Something fun," she told me.

"I'm sure I'll love it," I said and put it next to my place card.

Then Andrew, dressed like a royal prince, strolled up.

"This is your night, dah-ling," Andrew said as he kissed me on the cheek. "But it's mine too in a way, thanks to you," he whispered in my ear. "I decided to embrace my Rothschild heritage… Sotheby's has already sold my great-uncle's painting for eight hundred thousand dollars."

"Andrew, that is fabulous!" I gave him a big embrace.

I introduced Andrew to everyone at our table and then we sat down as the waiters whirred around us with dinner. Everyone looked gorgeous. We all were having a great time. Colleagues came up to congratulate me. It would have been my finest hour. If only David were here.

After dinner, John Peale approached the lectern, positioned so the three hundred guests could see and hear the director. "Ladies and gentlemen, welcome to the National Gallery of Art on this very special evening. First I would like to personally welcome Mrs. Lee Trevor of Whittington Plantation where *Lady in Waiting* lived for fifty years."

I helped Lee out of her chair and the Rotunda full of guests clapped.

"To Mrs. Trevor's right, is our own Millicent Clermont and Mrs. Trevor's good friend. Millicent's stellar efforts in helping to discover and return stolen art were courageous and even dangerous. Millicent, would you please stand up so we all can thank you."

I blushed involuntarily as I stood. I couldn't believe that everyone was applauding me. I quickly sat down.

"Mrs. Clermont, you must be very proud of your daughter. Would you please stand." My mother, in actress form, smiled and waved.

"Please help me welcome the granddaughter and grandson of the late Pierre and Pauline Alexander, Colette Alexander and her brother Jacques Alexander from Paris."

They stood and everyone applauded.

John Peale resumed his introductions. "Next to the Alexanders is Haywood Tabb, one of the world's finest art restitution lawyers."

Haywood stood halfway up and sat back down with a wave of his hand.

"Haywood Tabb, Millicent Clermont, and renowned art historian David Perry were nothing short of heroic," John continued. "It is because of their efforts that we celebrate tonight. Millicent and David solved the secret code in the overpainting and uncovered the treasure trove in Germany. Haywood and the F.B.I. brought art criminals to justice. Unfortunately David could not be here tonight. But please give all three of these remarkable individuals a round of applause for their outstanding and dangerous work."

I could barely hear the clapping. My heart constricted and my body sagged with the words, 'David could not be here tonight'. My mother subtly motioned me to sit up straight. How could Pet Wilde be here when his relatives were mentioned as criminals?

John resumed. "No doubt you recognize *Washington Post* writer Andrew Barlowe who has been doing a fantastic job in covering the story."

Andrew stood and gave a royal nod, beaming through his perpetual suntan.

"Now may I introduce Paul Morton, the National Gallery's curator of Northern Baroque Paintings," John said.

The audience clapped as Paul Morton joined John Peale at the lectern.

"It's an amazing experience to get to know a work of art by one of the greatest artists of all time," Paul said as he put on his horn-rimmed glasses. "It's an even greater experience to witness an art restitution case first hand that is a win-win situation for everyone involved. After the myriad scientific tests conducted on the painting and consultation with other Vermeer experts, we were happy to authenticate *Lady in Waiting* as an original painting by Johannes Vermeer."

John Peale and Paul Morton pulled away the black drapery covering Lee's painting. Anchored on an elaborate brass easel, the staged lightning perfectly caught the delicate colors of Lee's painting. I could hear expressions of appreciation throughout the room before it was filled with the sound of clapping hands and chairs scraping the marble floor as everyone stood up.

"As Paul said, this is an art restitution case that is a

win-win for all of us," John said, obviously relishing his role. "The agreement reached among all the parties was based on a similar case at the Chicago Art Institute. The fair market value of the painting is estimated by Christie's and Sotheby's at a hundred million dollars."

A gasp ran through the Rotunda and then everyone in the grand space became quiet. Then another gasp. A person had apparently fallen on the floor. Waiters rushed to the site of the accident. Ever on the alert, Haywood hurried there as well. The next thing we could see was a man being taken out of the room, a man with gray hair.

Haywood returned to the table, unruffled. "Pet Wilde was overcome with emotion and fainted. As duplicitous as the devil is, his years of evading his criminal activity may be coming to an end, if I have anything to do with it."

I hoped so. But the more I learned about the art world, the more I was convinced that it was full of dishonest cheats who operated unimpeded for years. If it weren't for people like Haywood....wait, did I say that?

John Peale had paused but then resumed as if nothing had happened. "We wish to thank Mrs. Trevor for conveying half of the painting to the Gallery. And we wish to thank Colette and Jacques Alexander for allowing the Gallery to buy, through private donations," the director emphasized, "the other half of the painting."

Everyone in the room applauded again. Collette and Jacques were beaming. They had found their family's long lost painting and would receive fifty million dollars. Lee was beaming. Her conveyance earned her a fifty million dollar tax credit and her tax problems were over.

"And happily for us, Vermeer's *Lady in Waiting,"* the director added, "will be on exhibit at the National Gallery for nine months of the year. The other three months it will be prominently displayed at the Louvre in Paris."

Everyone in the room stood and applauded once again. Our hands by that time were red from clapping and our mouths sore from smiling.

Diane Miles was right. I had faced the biggest professional challenge of my life. *Now Saturn, planet of lessons, move off my Uranus, planet of change. Come on, Venus, planet of love, conjunct my Jupiter, planet of abundance.*

My mother, Lee, Gabby, Haywood, Andrew, and the Alexanders embraced each other even though we were headed back to my townhouse for a champagne toast. What a glorious evening. Why was I not on top of the world?

As we strolled toward the door, I nearly lost my balance. A man who resembled David was walking toward us holding a huge bouquet of blue hydrangeas and pale pink peonies. My gosh, it *was* David. He had the most endearing look on his face.

"Millicent, I'm sorry I couldn't be here earlier. These are for you."

I accepted the gorgeous flowers with the pale blues

and pinks of Thoreau's tints of morning and evening. David took me in his arms and hugged me like he would never let me go.

"I've missed you, Millicent. I've missed you terribly," David spoke softly, his lips touching my ear. And then releasing me, his sapphire eyes looked into mine down to my soul. "I'm in a suite at the Four Seasons. Will you join me?"

"David, it's so great to see you." My eyes feasted on him. I held my tears in check. "You remember my mother..."

"Yes, Mrs. Clermont, it is so nice to see you again," David took her hand in both of his.

"And this is Mrs. Lee Trevor of Whittington," I beamed.

"It's an honor to meet you, Mrs. Trevor." David slightly bowed.

"And my best friend Gabby, and my neighbor Andrew Barlowe."

"It's great to meet you. Collette, Jacques, Haywood, wonderful seeing you." David said as they shook hands. "Would you care to come to the Four Seasons? I believe they have plenty of Veuve Clicquot and I would be delighted for all of you to be my guest. I can't think of a more perfect time to invite Millicent to accompany me to Venice."

"Venice?" I nearly dropped my bouquet.

"Yes," David explained. "A painting has been

discovered in a Venetian palace and the owner wants me to figure out its provenance."

"Millie, I definitely think you should go with David," my mother was the first to respond.

"I agree," Lee added. "You deserve a grand holiday."

"Let me check my schedule," Haywood joked. "I better be sure we can give you F.B.I. coverage."

"And then come to Paris on your way home," Colette said. "Jacques and I would love to throw a special party for you and David."

David and I stood side to side with an arm wrapped around the other's waist. Was this an illusion? Or was this real? My body, mind, and spirit sent me a message: "Yes, this is real."

Author's Note

Vermeer's Lady in Waiting is a work of fiction. The names, characters, places, and incidents are either the product of the author's imagination or are used fictitiously. Any resemblance to actual persons, living or dead, events, or locales is entirely coincidental.

The painting *Lady in Waiting* does not exist. If it did, it would look similar to one of the paintings illustrated in *Vermeer, The Complete Works*, by Arthur K. Wheelock, Jr., Curator of Northern Baroque Paintings at the National Gallery of Art. The resolution of the painting in this novel was based on an actual case at the Art Institute in Chicago. The heirs of Holocaust victims Friedrich and Louise Gutmann were paid for half of Edgar Degas' monotype *Landscape with Smokestacks* while the current owner, Daniel Searle, donated the other half to the Art Institute. [*The AMA Guide to Provenance Research*, page 105.]

Whittington Plantation is a figment of the author's imagination. However, historical references to Gloucester County are true. Haywood Tabb's ancestry is fictional but factually based. Plantations in Virginia owned as many as three thousand slaves per farm to work the fields pre-Civil War.

The "Wereth 11" refers to the eleven soldiers from the actual 333rd Field Artillery Regiment, a black battalion that the Nazis tortured, then killed near the town of Wereth, Belgium on December 17, 1944.

Evil exist in many forms. But surely one of its most horrific manifestations came during World War II through Adolf Hitler, Hermann Goering, and the Nazi party. Their cruel and inhuman treatment mostly of Jewish citizens is true. Their obliteration of lives and legacies through their greedy confiscation of art and their destruction of priceless cultural artifacts are tragically true.

Hitler did consult astrologer and hypnotist Erik Jan Hanussen to learn mass psychology, dramatic speaking, and crowd control. Erik Hanussen was later killed for having Jewish blood. Hitler's inner circle also consulted astrologers. Karl Krafft, who consulted Adolf Hess and Heinrich Himmler, was imprisoned and died in a concentration camp for his accurate predictions.

The Einsatzstab Reichsleiter Rosenberg (ERR) was the actual Nazi agency in charge of carte blanche confiscation of art and other valuable artifacts in Nazi-occupied countries. In France, Nazi looted art was taken to the Jeu de Paume museum in Paris. Goering and Hitler made several trips to the Jeu de Paume to select their personal favorites from the thousands of paintings and sculpture taken from Jewish art dealers and private residences.

Formed under President Roosevelt during World War II, the Monuments, Fine Arts, and Archives program, known as Monuments Men, was a group of approximately 350 men and women—museum directors, curators, art historians, and educators—who volunteered to track, protect, and repair cultural treasures. In the last year of the war, their heroic efforts led to the return of thousands of artistic and cultural treasures stolen by the Nazis.

When the war escalated, Nazis hid thousands of confiscated works of art in churches, castles, and salt mines. The Alt Aussee salt mine in Austria, where over 6,500 paintings and thousands of drawings, sculpture and other artwork were hidden, was the Monuments Men's largest and most important discovery. Alt Aussee turned out to be a good place to preserve priceless art because of its moderate temperatures (40 degrees to 48 degrees Fahrenheit) and low humidity.

Perhaps the most famous forger who ever lived, Han van Meegeren, did in fact forge many Vermeer paintings fooling experts and collectors alike. Van Meegeren was arrested for being a Nazi collaborator to whom he sold Dutch cultural treasures. He avoided a death sentence by admitting his forgeries and arguing that by tricking Goering into trading several Dutch paintings for his fake Vermeer, Van Meegeren was a hero not a criminal. Van Meegeren was sentenced to one year of prison for his fraudulent activity but died before serving any time.

The Hammerskins (also known as Hammerskin

Nation) are a worldwide white supremacist organization. On August 5, 2012, Wade Michael Page, a member of the Hammerskins, killed six people in a Sikh temple in Wisconsin. Stormfront, a website devoted to promoting prejudice and bigotry including Holocaust denial, also exists today. Stormfront's logo is a Celtic cross surrounded with the words "White Pride World Wide."

For further research on provenance, invest in *The AMA Guide to Provenance Research* co-authored by Nancy Yeide. It is highly readable and informative. For an overview of the Nazis' art greed, read Lynn Nicholas' The *Rape of Europa* and rent or download the film by the same title. The story of the Monuments Men is told and illustrated in *Rescuing DaVinci* by Robert Edsel.

To search the databases of Nazi looted art, click onto ERRproject.org, Lootedart.com, ArtLossRegister.com, ArtCommision.com, and Nepip.org (Nazi Era Provenance Internet Portal). Thousands of paintings, sculptures, and other valuable artwork stolen by the Nazis are still missing.

Acknowledgements

On September 11, 2001, my new job hung in the balance as I waited for National Gallery officials to approve my hiring as Senior Associate for Annual Giving. The 9-11 tragedy delayed it a day but then I began work the following Monday. It was a stunning time for anyone working in Washington. Shortly after, the Anthrax scare changed daily routines: mail was rerouted to a Maryland location where it was treated with chemicals. The discolored mail—including checks from donors—emitted an odor. Those who handled it wore rubber gloves. Mail is an integral part of fundraising so these unusual circumstances added to the challenge.

I will be forever grateful to my former colleagues at the National Gallery of Art. The Gallery is a magnificent place not only because of its world-class art but also because of its dedicated professionals who perpetuate the gift of Andrew Mellon under the watchful eye of Washington politics.

My special thanks to Franklin Kelly, Deputy Director, Arthur Wheelock, Curator of Northern Baroque Paintings, Ann Bigley Robertson, Exhibition Officer, Sarah Fisher, Senior Conservator and Head of Department of Painting Conservation, and especially Nancy Yeide, Head of Curatorial Records and Files, for their generous time and patience in helping me frame my novel.

My appreciation goes to Dennis Brack and the National Gallery for permission to use his stunning photograph for my book cover. Thank you, Jean Henry and Barbara Bernard for helping with that process. Thank you, Peter Huestis, for helping with the digital images of Vermeer's paintings.

I 'did not build' this novel by myself. My coterie consisted of talented writers in my critique group: Mary Price, Lark Baxter, Danelle Hall, Ken and Barbara Greer, Kristyn Reid, Maria Veres, Barbara Fretwell, Audrey Streetman, Beverly Roem, and Dale Acker. Catherine Miller, also a talented writer, editor, and friend helped with the numerous rewrites. They suffered through the many drafts and I thank them for their continued encouragement. Dr. Sandra Mayfield, thank you for freeing me to write with confidence. Kathe Birnbaum, Millicent Sukman, Laura Sandefer, and Nicole Barr, thank you for reading early drafts. Gail Chapman Haynes and Skipper Jones listened attentively to my rants. Rosalind Reeder jump-started the process when I really needed it. Neal Holland Duncan, thank you for adding color to my characters. For their affirmation of a novel on Nazi looted art and helpful suggestions, I thank Aviva Layton and Ken Sherman. Margaret Gaeddert, it was fun working with you on the interior design. Matt Goad, friend and designer extraordinaire, once more you have created a book cover that rocks.

Special appreciation and love go to my beautiful and smart eighty-seven-year-old mother for two gifts: one, taking me to the National Gallery of Art when I was in the seventh grade that began my love of art museums, and two, reading and re-reading my manuscript making invaluable suggestions and edits.

Connie, wherever you are, playing the harp no doubt, thank you for forty-five years of inspiration.

Lastly and most greatly, I am blessed with a brilliant husband who inexhaustibly supported and sustained me every frustrating and exhilarating step of this monumental experiment called a novel. Mike, I love you and we both know this book would not exist without you.

About the Author

Laurel "Lolly" Anderson's professional work as a lawyer then later as a development officer for the National Gallery of Art were invaluable in creating her first novel. *Vermeer's Lady in Waiting* and her other books, *How My Magic Refrigerator Sent Me to Paris Free* and *Aussie at the Skirvin Hilton*, are available on Amazon.com and Barnes&Noble.com and your local bookstore.

Visit her website: **www.LollyAnderson.net**

www.ingramcontent.com/pod-product-compliance
Lightning Source LLC
LaVergne TN
LVHW091033080826
845145LV00002B/469

* 9 7 8 0 9 8 1 9 3 7 6 8 7 *